On *Silverfish*

'The first thing…about this debut novel is its elegant lucidity—how carefully each word is chosen, each sentence written, how beautifully phrases are strung together to garland a narrative that is at the same time compelling, magical, public, private, and strewn with judiciously chosen fragments of memory…*Silverfish* is a brilliantly etched, haunting, intelligent first novel.'

– Hindustan Times

'A moving debut from a talented new voice.'

– Indian Express

'To Majumdar, words are almost supernatural—they shape our identity, our history and they fend off death.'

– Daily Star

The Scent of God

SAIKAT MAJUMDAR

**SIMON &
SCHUSTER**

London · New York · Sydney · Toronto · New Delhi

A CBS COMPANY

First published in India by Simon & Schuster India, 2019
A CBS company
Copyright © Saikat Majumdar, 2019
This edition published in 2019

The right of Saikat Majumdar to be identified as author of this work has been asserted by him in accordance with Section 57 of the Copyright Act, 1957.

1 3 5 7 9 10 8 6 4 2

Simon & Schuster India
818, Indraprakash Building,
21, Barakhamba Road,
New Delhi 110001

www.simonandschuster.co.in

HB ISBN: 978-93-86797-36-0
eBook ISBN: 978-93-86797-37-7

Typeset in India by SÜRYA, New Delhi

Printed and bound in India by Replika Press Pvt. Ltd.

Simon & Schuster India is committed to sourcing paper that is made from wood grown in sustainable forests and support the Forest Stewardship Council, the leading international forest certification organisation. Our books displaying the FSC logo are printed on FSC certified paper.

To the memory of Professor P. Lal
(1929–2010)

And for Wendell Mayo
teacher, editor, champion

The Magic Wrist

Whenever India played Pakistan, the villagers in Mosulgaon wanted India dead. For the boys, that was the best reason to watch cricket on TV. The village was just outside the walls of the hostel; their roars and firecrackers were real, an enemy of their own!

That Saturday, India was to play Pakistan. But even such excitement paled next to that of watching it in the common room of Bliss Hall. It was a dark festival. All eighty of them packed on the floor of the room, on the thick, ribbed carpet. The door was closed and weak sunlight filtered through the glass pane of the windows. Garish light flickered from the TV set perched on the table in front.

The boys wanted to shout and scream but for Kamal Swami sitting on a chair at the back. Kamal Swami was unbeatable on the cricket field, he aimed like Arjun. His saffron robes flapped wildly in the wind when he bowled, and before you blinked, the ball blew up the wicket like a child's toy-house. But he rarely spoke during match-screenings, only once in a while to make a rare forecast whether a batsman would stay or get out. And he was always right, so that scared the boys a little.

In the darkness, the common room became a maddening place. No one could see anything. It was like a movie theatre. The blue flannels on the screen and the frenzy of cheering spectators on the stands, all that was visible in the common room of boys who cheered in whispers. The crowd drove them crazy, for the match was happening in Peshawar and the Pakistanis wanted to drown the Indian batsmen in their fierce war-cry. From time to time the boys wanted to smash the TV screen, claw at the brute Pakistanis who waved massive green-crescent flags like weapons at the heroic Indian batsmen who fought their killer bowlers.

'Cut their dicks off,' Bora whispered softly at the TV.

'Dicks slit already,' Asim Chatterjee roared. 'Bloody mullahs!'

'Firecrackers going off at Mosulgaon,' someone whispered. 'They cheer when Pakistani bowlers get a wicket.'

They lived and breathed with this village. One could see the thatched huts from the rooms of the C Block, and if they stared hard they could also spot muddy-looking women bathing. The villagers hated the ashram and they wanted Pakistan to rub the noses of the Indian team in the dirt.

'Slit-dicks!' Asim Chatterjee roared again.

'Asim!' His name flew and hit Chatterjee like a thunderbolt from the back. Kamal Swami's voice always pierced like an arrow. Chatterjee crumpled up like a withered flower. He looked big and burly and already had hairy temples and upper lips but it was easy to crack him as under the loud body of a bully there was always shame, the shame of hairy whiskers and upper lips in Class 7 and the reminder that he was a man among children.

But Kamal Swami never had to say much.

Silence thickened in the common room, the TV buzzing alone. The flag-waving Pakistani crowd was gone, vanished into the television and far away in Peshawar. Anirvan glanced to his left. Kajol sat staring at the TV. His face said nothing. The Swami's voice had not touched him. He never rested till the last equation on his homework was solved to perfection and nobody ever found a balled-up sock under his bed. Was he really watching the match? Or just looking at the TV because they were all supposed to?

To watch the Pakistani leg-spinner Abdul Qadir was to die laughing, but to face him on the pitch was to face death. Balls pitched at perfect length and spinning up to a foot to knock the bails off the stumps. A deadly googly where the ball struck the direction opposite to where it was supposed to go. He danced like a cripple trying to twist at the disco and it was painful to watch a man do such things to his body. But they had stopped laughing as the ball that came out of that dance was an arrow of death for the batsman.

The silence became more pointed. Watching Qadir was a bizarre kind of a delight. He began his twisted dance to the wicket and the whole room leaned forward. Anirvan's weight rested on palms splayed on the carpet on either side, ready to attack. The ball fell at the perfect length before the leg stump, and the batsman tried to drive it towards long-on. The ball caught the edge of the bat and shot at the off-stump like a snake's tongue. The hawk at the slip caught the ball and the Pakistani team howled like a pack of wolves. A gasp went up in the dark room and Anirvan clenched his fingers to feel Kajol's palm in his own. It was a soft and small palm, almost like a baby's. The anxiety of the moment was a disease and one had to share it.

A curly-haired sixteen-year-old boy had appeared to face the guile of Abdul Qadir. His name was Sachin Tendulkar and he had raked up some massive innings in domestic tournaments. But he was just a boy and the devious Qadir would slaughter him soon. They waited.

Anirvan had not let go of Kajol's hand. It was beginning to feel strange as the moment couldn't last forever, the moment when one slapped his neighbour's thigh or clenched a hand in excitement, but he held Kajol's palm and sensed the moisture in it, the moisture coating his bony knuckles.

He was a boy really, this Sachin Tendulkar, a curly-haired boy who could perhaps play in the older boys' school team. It was absurd and delightful to see him in the massive cricket gear—the pad and the helmet and the heavy bat, among these real and famous cricketers. The boys were just happy that Waqar Younis—the deadly paceman—was not there to draw blood with his bouncers. He would come back soon but the trickster Qadir would happily send the boy back to the safety of the pavilions long before that.

Anirvan unfurled each of Kajol's fingers slowly inside his palm, like he was playing a secret game of numbers with his digits. Kajol had smooth, well-trimmed nails. Anirvan ran his fingers over them and imagined his tiny nail-cutter tucked away carefully inside his desk where everything was arranged like a library catalogue. He was the kind of boy who never trimmed his nails on a day he was not supposed to, like a Thursday, or the day of the week he was born, just as his mother had told him. One who set aside two days in the week when he clipped them after his bath, when they were soft.

Anirvan's heart beat wildly. Sachin Tendulkar took guard to face Abdul Qadir. Anirvan caressed Kajol's fingers, feeling the spot behind his knuckles where the skin wrinkled, the spot below it where tiny hairs had sprouted, so tiny and so little, he was almost hairless.

Qadir did his fatal dance. The ball pitched and spun madly. The boys wanted to close their eyes and not see the terrifying sight of the bails flying off the stumps.

Swiftly, the curly-haired boy changed into a battle-stallion and hooked it wildly over mid-wicket. A sixer!

The boys gasped and almost forgot to cheer. And then they cheered, a wisp of sorrow in their voices. What a spunky boy! He will kick before they kill him. *Soon.*

Anirvan squeezed Kajol's hand. His fingers slid back, caressed his wrist, the baby bone awake on the corner, the veins of his pulse that made up the soft belly of the wrist. It was his to play with. It did not question Anirvan's claim on it, doing whatever he wanted to do with it. He did not dare to look at Kajol but knew he was staring at the TV. Did he resent having to watch cricket? Perhaps the rowdiness of the Pakistani spectators and the rowdiness of Asim Chatterjee made him wince.

The camera focused on Abdul Qadir, returning to his dancing run-up. A smile danced on his lips. A cheerful snake. He would now kill the boy, split his stumps wide open. Bora closed his eyes and said something under his breath. It was some kind of a prayer. It was odd to see Bora pray, as if he were ill and had no idea what he was doing.

The ball pitched right on the middle stump and spun in the wrong direction. A googly that would sting the leg stump. Smoothly, the curly haired boy pulled the ball over long leg. Out of the field and out of the world!

Who was this Sachin Tendulkar? Who was this boy, really? What kind of guile had made his wrists?

Anirvan's heart leaped. Kajol squeezed his fingers, quickly, clumsily. Anirvan glanced at him through the corner of his eye; he looked straight at the TV. Where did he have his heart? In Peshawar or with the algebra left unsolved in his room? Somewhere else?

And then Sachin Tendulkar sent Qadir outside the stadium for a third time. His wrist turned like the arc of a revolving planet. The spectators were quiet, in sudden mourning. The boys' chests hurt with pride and were about to explode. The firecrackers had died out there in Mosulgaon.

Qadir was smiling. The bastard was game!

Everything felt right. Anirvan wanted to bring Kajol's delicate wrist to his mouth, suck his soft baby fingers one by one. There was an ache in his loins. Everything was taut.

'Take that you split-dicks!' Asim Chatterjee howled.

'Turn off the TV!' Kamal Swami's voice struck out like a slap across the room.

Anirvan pulled out his hand sharply from Kajol's.

Before they knew it, Sunondo Dey stood up in the front row and turned off the television. He loved to follow the vilest orders of the Swami. He hated to see his classmates happy.

The boy with the magic wrist was gone.

Cane

Kamal Swami hit them where it hurt. He took the TV away right when the firecrackers were dying down in Mosulgaon.

The Swami never made a mistake. He had taught Anirvan so much. How to craft a deadly backhand smash across the ping-pong table. How to blow the conch before prayer.

The first day he tried, the conch had sucked all the air from Anirvan's lungs but no music had come out. It had made a noise like a fart. He had puffed up his cheeks again and blown hard into the curled mouth of the large white shell. Nothing.

That day, he had asked Nath to let him do it. Nath had looked confused. 'Huh?' It was hard to make out emotions on Nath's dark and knotted face. He was the tribal boy with spunk in his lungs. It was his duty to blow the conch at prayer every day.

'You can't,' Nath had said.

'But I can.' Anirvan had argued.

The song of the conch was the beginning of prayer. The boys became quiet the moment the conch was blown.

Anirvan's lungs were about to burst. He felt a hand touch his right shoulder.

'Here,' Kamal Swami said softly. 'Give it to me.'

Anirvan felt his heart stop. Kamal Swami was the hostel warden of Bliss Hall. The silent monk. Nobody heard him as he never wore shoes or slippers indoors. You never knew if he was faraway or right behind you. The boys fell quiet the moment he walked into the room.

The Swami lifted the conch to his lips. His saffron chador, neatly folded on his right shoulder, creased lightly. The music came. An arrogant booming wail. It wouldn't stop. Not even the tribal boy Nath had such force in his lungs.

The Swami paused.

'Turn your lips into an O,' he whispered. He reached out with his fingers, touched Anirvan's lips, shaping them like he was trying to curl open the petals of a flower. He smelled of incense and cardamom, and his saffron robe was like a seawave.

'Push hard while you blow.

Like this.'

He blew again. And again. Long wails swam out like fragrant war-cries. They swirled around the prayer hall, flew past the long, L-shaped corridor of the hostel, swung around the rooms of the boys, and floated in waves over the wide green ashram lawns.

Anirvan's lips felt numb.

The Swami stepped inside the prayer hall. Quietly, Anirvan followed him.

Inside, there were eighty of them. Eighty eleven-year-old boys draped in coarse cotton chador, seated in drowsy rows filling the hall, shrouded in the fine white haze of incense.

They were half asleep. They had sleepwalked outdoors at daybreak for their PT class in white t-shirts, khaki shorts and white running shoes which Sushant Kane said made them look like young prisoners. But it was Sushant Kane's older brother, Prashant Kane, who stood in the football field and called out their names to make sure that nobody missed PT. They ran around the field four times and did those impossible arches—stretched out behind and touched the ground with both hands. Anirvan could never do it.

If you missed PT you had to do an arch while Prashant Kane slashed a cane on the soft hind part of your legs. If that made you lose your balance you had to do the whole thing all over again ... and again till you could arch quietly while being caned. The monks said your mind should be beyond touch while your body was in pain. Sometimes the boys screamed. But most of the time they stayed quiet.

When they marched back into their hostels and tied the chadors over the khaki shorts they were too tired to take off, most of them were still in the haze of sleep. By seven o'clock they were inside the prayer hall. Nobody could talk inside the hall. If Tridib, the biology teacher, heard a boy speak there would be such a smack on his temple that his head would sing throughout prayer. But you were lucky if you were caught by the biology teacher. If you were unlucky, Kamal Swami might see you.

Kamal Swami never beat a boy if he heard him whisper or giggle during prayer. He stared at him with dead eyes. Then he would move his jaws slowly as if he had something to say. But he never said anything—just nodded his head from side to side. It made the boy feel dirty throughout the day, sometimes, for days afterwards, till the Swami called him to his room alone and spoke softly about how the mind was a brat of a child and the best way to discipline it was to simply let go, step beyond it, and watch its antics like he lived outside it.

Something stirred in their sleep-drugged bodies as Kamal Swami entered the prayer hall. They straightened their backs, just the way they were told to sit in meditation. Their spines felt the rhythm of the Swami's toes muffled inside his socks. He moved through Bliss Hall silent and shoeless, just in these soft socks, sliding through in the prayer hall, the dining hall, or the boys' rooms. It was the best reason for the boys to keep the floors clean and smooth, like a shiny coin they liked to spit on and polish.

Anirvan found peace when the Swami sat down. The Swami's skin glowed; his saffron robes had a fresh clean smell and a whiff of cardamom. He was like a prayer hall that walked.

'Leave your mind, swim out of it, and watch it wander,' the Swami always said.

Anirvan felt his whole being leave his body, float away on a light breeze, linger on the angular bones of the boy sitting next to him, whitened by the prayer chador flung over his body. Kajol was thin, and looked thinner under the thin cotton chador.

'Watch it like a fish bobbing in the water, a trivial, colourful thing that is no longer a part of you.'

Kajol always sat next to him during prayer. Kamal Swami had asked the two of them to sit on the right hand corner at the back of the hall, close to him.

Anirvan watched his body breathe. It was no longer his body. It pumped in and out like a lifeless machine. He was a wisp of smoke that floated away, like a genie escaping a magic lamp.

There was a single drop of life left in his body. Right around his left knee which touched Kajol's bony right knee. Throughout prayer, their knees were glued, afraid to breathe and stir, lest they lose each other.

Sleepwalk

The night of the semi-finals, Anirvan went to bed with the memory of the cricket match. He curled up with it like a child curls up with his soft toy. And so he slept, and so every night after that. It was a snatch of the day he could kiss and hug to sleep.

Kajol had said something. It was as if he had used real words. The boy who rarely spoke. Anirvan had thought he would never speak to him. Not even after the silent talk across the corridor, the day before the Class 7 half-yearly exams.

Walking to memorize was so hard. It was painful. Anirvan had tried to deny it for a while; but then he couldn't any longer. He was no bright spark. He had wandered into the school debate team but he struggled at the exams. His classmates could crack algebra equations in their sleep. And they never slept because they studied eighteen hours a day, combed their hair perfectly, and wore neatly washed and pressed shirts to school every day. Some of them were also good-looking and fair-complexioned and so the monks liked them. They always got the rooms right next to that of the hostel warden.

Anirvan had started out okay but sank quickly in the

midst of this pointless explosion of brilliance. The boys were nice but studies were a mean football field where people hid brute force under a smile. One could tell from the textbooks and notebooks bound in silken brown paper, the name-labels with name, class and section number sketched with love, the pencils sharpened pointy-perfect and the shiny geometry tools with no shadow of dust on them.

Then there were the heavy walking subjects. Books which needed to be memorized, and memorizing never happened unless you walked up and down the corridors. History, geography, literature, subjects which no one really cared about but they couldn't let them drag their averages down. Even biology and chemistry, which were important but needed a lot of mugging. So every month, the week before the monthly tests, a silent procession appeared on the block-corridors, quiet, lost figures walking with copies of *Our Living Planet*, *The History of India*, and *Life Science* pressed against the chest, eyes closed, muttering darkly.

Wednesday morning before the half-yearly exam was the time for home study. Anirvan sat in the corridor with the life science textbook on his lap. It was a sign that he had given up. The maze of scientific names and the mating habits of salmon. Did they live in the sea and come up to the river to spawn? Or did they live in the ocean or swim to the river to breed? It was all slipping away. If a boy wanted to learn, he walked. The monks knew that and stared at the boys from the distance when they passed. If a boy looked sleepy and crouched on the block or went into his room to sit on his bed, they came in and rapped his head.

But it was impossible to walk with the salmon as they moved back and forth between salt and sweet water. Anirvan sat down and stared at the shawls trailing past him, the rubber flip-flops that dragged along slowly. That was when he first sensed Kajol pass him. His black shawl went past Anirvan like a dark, warm film with fur that looked alive and silvery at places. Kajol was a quiet boy, small and dark like kohl, but with a delicate face that looked like it had been carefully sculpted. He looked younger than most students in their class.

He walked slowly. It looked like the large shawl was almost weighing him down. He was lost in a book. He was a good student, quiet and hardworking, and his handwriting was dreamlike. When he finished equations on the blank sheets of the mathematics exercise book it looked like calligraphy. He wrote slowly, like he was painting a picture.

Anirvan looked up as he passed, and Kajol glanced down at him. The air was heavy with the gloom of the examination, and they didn't know each other well. Kajol wasn't really friendly with anyone. But he seemed to like Anirvan; his eyes often hovered around him. Every now and then Anirvan looked up to feel the stillness of his stare. Kajol always sat to his right in class, a row ahead of him, and while looking at the back of his neck Anirvan felt Kajol knew that his eyes were there. Strangely, Anirvan wanted him to know. There was no shame of getting caught; Kajol couldn't actually see him. But every now and then, if someone said something at the back, Kajol turned and stared at Anirvan. Anirvan quickly looked away but always longed to look back. When he did, Kajol was still staring, as if he was talking to him in silence.

A few minutes passed and Anirvan floated along with the spawning salmon. Kajol passed again. Anirvan knew it from the smooth black shawl and the blue rubber flip-flops. He looked up and Kajol glanced at him but quickly looked into his book again. His flip-flops made a lazy, squishy kind of noise on the floor. He dragged his feet as he walked, very slowly, as if he would much rather be still but had been pushed into an inertia of motion by the rhythm of the walking flock. He had lean legs. There was a small scar under his right knee. Was it fresh or old? Anirvan wanted to reach out and trace it with his finger.

Did he slow down a little more when he passed Anirvan? Perhaps just a little? Anirvan wondered. Kajol was now on the other side of the corridor, walking back towards him. Anirvan glanced at him; he was looking at Anirvan. Their eyes touched for a while and suddenly Anirvan felt his heart pound. Kajol walked past him, dragging his flip-flops. It was a delicious kind of lethargy. He didn't look at Anirvan while passing by him but walked all the way to the end of the block. But the moment he turned, he glanced at Anirvan again. This time, Anirvan looked away. He'd been looking at him for too long.

His eyelashes were beautiful and he had an intense way of looking at you, almost a savage way, which felt uncanny because he was such a quiet boy with dreamy handwriting and high scores in every subject. He could explain crop rotation on the Deccan Plateau without batting an eyelash so you never noticed how beautiful they were till he looked at you.

But it was as if it never happened, as if nothing was happening even as they looked into each other's eyes, staring, staring, as he walked away, drawing Anirvan's gaze as if by invisible strings, gazing at him over the blue cover of *Our Living Planet*, vanishing at the end of the block and looking up the moment he turned around. He was such a serious boy with delicate lips. It was a secret impossible to bear. Anirvan sensed a flush of heat swim through his body. What were they doing? Was it wrong?

Ageless

'You have trained your grandson beautifully,' Kamal Swami told Anirvan's grandmother, suddenly brightening the afternoon. She had put on a new white sari that made her look more like a wife than a widow, and she had pulled the aanchal of the sari low over her head.

You have trained your grandson beautifully! That's the very first thing Maharaj told her. She would repeat it for months afterwards! Maharaj, the King; the saffron men were kings because they owned nothing, because they had given up this world.

'If a boy becomes a monk,' she had told Anirvan since he was a child, 'seven generations before him, and seven generations after attain nirvana.'

Her eyes glistened.

'Seven before and seven after, fourteen in all. Free from the cycle of life and death and rebirth!'

'Saffron is the true absence of colour,' she said. 'It comes *after* white.'

Smiling, she would tell Anirvan, 'Become a monk. Then our spirits will be free. Mine when I die. Your grandfather's spirit remains trapped in the cycle of karma. He will be free.'

She would tell him again later. And later again.

'He has your touch,' Kamal Swami told her, smiling. 'Made in the same mould.'

'My touch?' She smiled back, 'What do you know about my touch?'

'I know,' he smiled again. 'All there is to know.'

The seventy-two-year-old woman had put on a new sari that had sat untouched in her cupboard for decades, to make her feel clean enough to visit the ashram where her grandson lived. She only needed a little help from Anirvan and his father to walk into Kamal Swami's office in Bliss Hall—just a little—because she was so eager. She had gone around the table and touched the Swami's feet, bringing the dust of his feet back to her head. It was strange to see her do that to a man younger than her, by many years. How old was Kamal Swami? Thirty, maybe? The monk with shiny cheeks and lean and fast legs that shot through loose saffron robes on the cricket field. The man who could move like lightning without breaking a sweat?

But anybody could touch the feet of a saffron-clad monk, perform pranaam like you did to an elder, even if they were younger than you. 'They have no age, the monks,' people said. They did not belong to this world.

In his smooth saffron robe, he was ageless. The pure and smooth lotus, just as his name said. Lotus Swami, the Lord Lotus. Smooth and green on the cheeks. Hairy on his pale, sinewy arms that hit the ball outside the cricket stadium with the bald stump of a child's bat. He would always slouch a bit afterwards, and smile, almost in embarrassment, as if he was ashamed of using his superman force in a children's game.

But Anirvan felt his whole body was afloat, in a warm, bubbly fluid that bathed his ears and turned them red. It was such a beautiful smile. Kamal Swami had teeth like specks of a white flower, and suddenly the force left his body and he became a soft and blushing boy who wanted to hand the bat to another boy and go back to being a monk, hide his agile cricketer body in the billowy saffron robe. Desperately, Anirvan wanted to touch him, become him.

There was something about the ashram that, Anirvan knew, was like lying on his grandmother's bed, her fingers parting the curls of his hair.

The best part of his childhood still lay there, listening to her stories.

The two gods of the trinity—Vishnu the sustainer of the universe, and Shiva, the destroyer—were opposite characters.

Shiva is kind of a crazy god, happy and drunk but with a heart of gold. He becomes furious and dances to destroy the world. Then he is kind again, and gives whatever his devotees want.

'Vishnu is a million times craftier, far harder to please,' she said. 'The more you love him the more he makes you suffer. Only the greatest of the devotees survive.' She smiled at Anirvan. 'When they are on the brink of destruction, Vishnu comes to them, glowing in blue.'

She told him the stories of two young boys. Dhruva and Prahlad. Dhruva left his royal home at the age of five to sit alone in a forest to seek Lord Vishnu through prayer. He swayed the universe with his devotion and in the end the Lord appeared before him in his blue glory.

Prahlad was born of bad blood, of a cruel demon father who hated Vishnu and wanted to destroy the gods. Prahlad loved Vishnu and prayed to him all the time. His father tried to kill him, get him burned and bitten by snakes and eaten by fierce animals, but no danger could touch him. He sat in prayer for his dream-god, Vishnu, while the Lord appeared as half-man and half-lion and killed his demon father.

If you loved Vishnu, you suffered. If you loved Vishnu deeply, you suffered terribly. Vishnu loved to see his devotees suffer, as did his human avatar, Krishna, the mischievous blue lover. You had to love the pain, and sing for him, like Queen Meera, who called herself Krishna's lover and suffered the rage of her royal husband.

Anirvan's grandmother was a widow and she wore the widow's white but Krishna was her lover and so he gave her a life filled with pain. The world became cruel to her soon after Anirvan's grandfather passed away and she was left to the care of her uncaring son. But her suffering made her cry and smile and then cry more tears of joy as if she knew it was Krishna's love for her. Krishna made her his own by making her suffer many years of pain.

Dhruva's devotion to Vishnu was so unflinching that it made him into a star. The Dhruva Tara, the North Star, the heavenly body that shone in the night sky in the same spot throughout the year. Lost sailors fixed their masts by looking at the bright white light up in the northern sky.

Could Anirvan be like them?

Yes, he could. He was special. He was pure of heart and had a pure mind. He could recite the hymns, and he knew all the stories from the Puranas. In a trembling voice, she told him the stories of the boy-devotees. His eyes became moist.

Life in the monastery was a fragrant, musical dream. It was a blaze of saffron that raged across the football field, black hair matted on pale, sweaty arms, eyes that laughed and loved you so much that you had nightmares of losing the love.

A Dreamhole

Sushant Kane was going to destroy everything. In class he recited poems he'd written, love poems like these:

The bleating ram of my soul
Is tied to the lamp-post of your heart

Such poems caused the boys pain. They did not know whether to laugh or cry. Was it poetry or a joke?

Sushant Kane looked so hip that it was absurd. He was a skinny man with hollow cheeks covered with acne-marks and a trimmed beard. He was the Class 7 English teacher and the debate coach. He wore tight shirts and trousers that flapped loosely around the ankles. It was easy to imagine him in dark sunglasses even though no one had ever seen him wearing any.

He spoke about everything outside the ashram—city buses and plays, exhibitions and advertisements, movies and books they didn't know could exist. He made it all sound real, even though they knew they were stories. Like this play he saw last Saturday in the city, where a lone woman played all the roles. It was the story of The Mahabharata, told by Draupadi, the wife of the five princes, how she was given away as property lost in a wager over a game of dice, fought over, insulted and attacked. There was no one else on stage the whole two hours. She even played an army and battle stallions.

Sushant Kane was a mathematician of grammar. Everything about him was pointed, his cheekbones, the end of his beard, the rhythm of his poems and the chalk with which he split complex and compound sentences on the board. Complex sentences into a principal and a subordinate clause, compound sentences into two principal clauses with a finite verb each. Nothing else existed.

He was one of the ashram stories. There were three Marathi brothers—Sushant, Prashant and Ashant—who were adopted by the monks. They were probably orphaned or something like that, nobody really knew how the story began or trailed off. Prashant was a brute with a balding head who ran the early morning PT and late-afternoon naval cadet training drill as if he was following Hitler's orders. Ashant was popular with the sporty boys; he was a lighthearted loafer who coached the football team and zipped around the ashram on his snazzy yellow Yamaha motorbike. Most of his fans had been won by the bike. Ashant wore sunglasses while riding the bike and usually forgot to take them off while at lunch in the hostel dining hall.

Sushant Kane was different. He was pale like his brothers but different in every other way. He wasn't well-built like them. He was too thin; his limbs were long twigs. Prashant and Ashant were ashram boys; they breathed its air. They sang Sanskrit hymns and tortured the students till they got the marching drill exactly right for the Independence Day and Republic Day parades. They were big brawny men who became little boys before the Great Monk—the Secretary of the ashram. Sushant Kane did not change. His acne-marked cheeks wrinkled the same way before the monks as before the boys in his seventh standard English class. Neither the boys nor the monks knew for sure if the trimmed beard hid a kind or a cruel smile. That's probably why he got the nickname Senior Kane, even though he was the middle brother.

Senior Kane, SrK.

SrK belonged to the ashram, like his brothers. And yet, unlike them, he did not belong here. He made the world outside real and fantastic at the same time. For his brothers, there was no world outside.

He talked a lot. He spoke slowly. Sometimes you felt he was asking you to get out and run.

The boys' rooms did not have fans. They spent most of the year in these rooms that had large windows but no electric fan. They went home for summer vacations during the hottest weeks of the year. At home, they could lie on their beds and stare at the electric fans whirring overhead. There were heavy, old-time fans that swallowed the entire ceiling and became a blur; and new, tiny white ones that were like cute, deadly animals swooshing out swirls of air that felt absurd coming out of their little bodies. Even table fans like grim night nurses.

Sometimes, after the boys came back to their hostels

after summer vacation, they stayed up late into the
night and chatted dreamily about the different kinds of
fans they had seen that vacation. At homes, in doctor's
waiting rooms, even in railway waiting rooms. The night
air in their rooms was deadly still. It was still summer.
Sometimes they could smell monsoon in the air that crept
up from the Bay of Bengal down south, rainy wind on its
way to Calcutta further north. Sometimes they dreamt
so hard that the cool air entered their rooms and danced
softly over their beds.

Daytime was different. The boys barely spent any
time in their rooms. They flew from one hall to another:
prayer hall to study hall to dining hall. And school and
the football field. Football was sacred as the young
saffron prophet had said that you'll be a lot closer to
God if you played football than if you read The Gita.
Always in motion, the boys felt wind on their skin. But
there was to be no fan in the boys' rooms. It was the
time to build character and the breeze from electric fans
was an indulgence. The monks liked the boys sweaty and
breathless. That was the true path of Yoga.

Something strange happened to Anirvan every time he
walked past Sushant Kane's room at the end of their block
in Bliss Hall. Whenever Sushant Kane was inside, the door
was bolted shut. They saw him quietly walk across the
block, a white prayer chador flung across his slim-fitting
shirt, walk into his room and bolt the door. He went to
the prayer hall. Every teacher had to go.

Anirvan walked up and down the block balcony
during Sunday morning room study. He was reading *Our*

Living Planet, their Geography textbook. Ontario, Erie, Michigan... Ontario, Superior... Ontario. The paragraph on agricultural produce. He had to memorize that whole chapter. The trick was to read it once, and then try to repeat it without looking at the book, and then read it again. And repeat the whole thing, and keep repeating the sentences till you could say the whole paragraph without looking at the book. Whoever could remember would go far in life, the monks always said.

Anirvan hadn't realized that he had stopped walking. He was remembering furiously. There was corn, and there was...what else was there? Suddenly his feet wouldn't budge. A blast of cool air hit his face. He looked up and stared at Sushant Kane's window. It was open. Inside, it was dark, and quiet but for a steady whirring sound. The electric fan spread cool air inside, and every time he came close to the window it blasted his face.

It was July but they had only a few days of rain. The leaves on the trees had stopped moving and the sun glared everywhere. The boys had to keep the windows of their rooms open or otherwise they would die but the open windows made the rooms hotter and many of the boys just lay with thin wet towels on their faces which dried up in a few minutes. On these weekends, they missed the coolness of the school and study halls. The prayer hall, with its heavy fans and dark curtains, was heaven.

The window revealed a dreamhole. Dark and cool and full of the steady music of the electric fan. Anirvan could stand there forever. He wanted to thrust his face against the bars and let them leave dents on his cheeks. He stood

close and breathed deeply. Cigarettes. He couldn't see
Sushant Kane through the window but could hear the
rustle of paper.

Kamal Swami did not have an electric fan in his room.
The monks never did. They smiled through the pain. For
them, it was no pain. Though everybody knew that the
house of Atal Swami—the secretary of the Mission—was
fully air-conditioned and also had a swimming pool
because there were many foreign visitors who came and
stayed in his house. The boys had never seen that house
but they knew, especially about the white women who
swam in the huge blue swimming pool. But the teachers
all had fans in their rooms. They were not monks. They
were human beings.

The boys had never been inside the room of any of
the teachers. Standing before Sushant Kane's window,
Anirvan knew why.

Room 25, Block 5. The room was there but not really
there. It smelled different. Of cool air and cigarette smoke
and darkness at noon. Standing in front of the room,
Anirvan knew things were scattered and unkempt inside.
He peered inside the room. The smoke smell hit him with
a coarse sweetness. He felt dazed and knew that he had
left the hostel already. He was home.

Home was the whir of the fan but also the rough
sweetness of the cigarette smoke. Sushant Kane was
nothing like Anirvan's father but they smoked the same
cigarette. Charminar. His father was not bony like Sushant
Kane but smooth and pale and delicate. Everything about
him was round and soft and slow, versus Sushant Kane's

clicking pointiness. But they smoked the same cigarette. As Anirvan flattened his nose against the window bars, he caught the silhouette of Sushant Kane's outstretched legs. He was lying on the bed in his pajamas smoking a cigarette. Anirvan's father did that too. The smoke twirled around in the dark and quickly got lost in the breeze of the fan.

He walked along the corridor, remembering the paragraph about grain production in the Great Lakes Region. He hummed the lines as he walked. His feet picked up the rhythm of the song and his flip-flops dragged to the beat on the floor.

But he slowed down every time he came close to Sushant Kane's room. He thirsted for the blast of cool air and the bitterness of cigarette smoke. He paused again.

There was a click at the door.

'What's up?' Sushant Kane's voice floated out. 'Come in.'

Anirvan stepped inside. His eyes were riveted on the red spark that glowed in the darkness. As Anirvan walked inside, Sushant Kane stubbed it out on the ashtray. A wisp of blue smoke wafted away.

Anirvan stared at the ceiling fan. Sushant Kane followed his eyes and looked above, staring for a moment. Quickly, Anirvan's eyes closed.

'Come, sit,' Sushant Kane pointed Anirvan to a chair under the fan.

Then he stepped out of the room.

The dark room was now faintly lit up by the light from the half-open door. It looked like an old library.

Books were everywhere. On the shelves and heaped on the table and the bed. And newspapers. Piles and piles of newspapers. Where did he get them? No newspaper ever came to the ashram.

Sushant Kane came back. His face was wet. Water dripped from his hair.

'It's burning outside,' he said.

He stared blankly in Anirvan's direction, at his hair being ruffled by the wind of the fan. His voice softened.

'Ah, the exam warrior!' He looked at Anirvan as if he could finally see him.

Anirvan smiled a little.

'You were sharp in class this week,' Sushant Kane said with a mild frown. 'People rarely see what odd fun language can be.'

Anirvan nodded. He felt overpowered by the breeze of the fan. He felt if he tried to speak the words would fly away.

'But grammar's just a game,' Sushant Kane said. 'That's not how you master a language.'

'But you know that.' He added, staring at Anirvan. 'You speak beautifully. That's the most important gift.'

He did? But he did, indeed he did! Anirvan's body throbbed.

'I...I,' he stammered. 'I really like your class.'

Sushant Kane nodded. In that half-darkness, he looked like a ghost.

Sushant Kane's class was in the afternoon the next day. Afternoons felt sated and sleepy, the right time for his classes. It was not the right time for the important subjects, like mathematics or physics or biology. But Anirvan liked SrK's English grammar class on Monday afternoons. They were precise and angular, like SrK's cheekbones. But they were not real math; Anirvan couldn't have solved them if they were. They were just a game. Being good at English grammar was a useless skill. It had nothing to do with real merit, which was about being good at physics, algebra or biology, real subjects that created success in life.

But that afternoon Anirvan felt a whir of laughter behind the cracking of clauses. Sushant Kane did not look his usual sharp and angular self. There was something cool about him, like there were ways of beating the afternoon heat that his body knew but he couldn't tell them. Anirvan felt a smile dance through SrK's beard. Was it a smile or something else? It was strange as he was not someone who smiled much. But he said things that made the boys smile.

Anirvan spoke a lot in class that day. Suddenly, his heart beat faster. He tossed the clauses back and forth with SrK as the rest of the class stared at them, looking amused and bored at the same time. But SrK rarely looked at Anirvan. He never looked at anyone, even while talking to them. But Anirvan hoped that he would look at him.

Rajeev Lochan Sen stared at them for a long time, looking back and forth between Sushant Kane and Anirvan. He was a thin boy with sharp wit and a girlish voice from a hilly town in north Bengal. He had clever things to say in every class, things which had little to do with the subjects being taught. He sang beautifully and had a voice carved with affection.

'Does clause analysis make you clever?' He sounded lost as he asked the question.

'Not the way chess does,' said Asim Chatterjee, the big boy who had failed a few classes and dropped down to theirs. Nobody had ever seen him play chess, and he hated clause-analysis. 'Chess makes you the smartest.'

Anirvan laughed. Kajol turned and stared at him. He sat across the aisle. Kajol had large eyes that looked moist when he stared at someone, and he looked at Anirvan every now and then, their eyes meeting. Anirvan wanted to look away and look back at the same time.

'Chess.' Bora, a dark and dangerous boy from Guwahati, whistled. 'Chess.' He studied Hindi instead of Bangla and hence had that posh-dumb accent when he spoke Bangla. 'Not true! Algebra is for the sharpest people.'

'Cracking clauses makes you better at cracking clauses.' Sushant Kane stared at them. 'Playing chess makes you a better chess player. If you're sharp at algebra, that's what you are sharp at.'

The boys waited. This could begin another poem about rams and lamp-posts.

'There is no cosmic intelligence,' he smiled through his sharp beard and Anirvan imagined beautiful smoke-rings curling out of his nose. 'Every skill is just that. The skill at doing just that thing.'

'No such thing,' he said, savouring his joke the way he savoured his love poetry. He glanced at Anirvan for the fraction of a second but quickly, his eyes were lost. 'Nothing cosmic at all.'

It was a strange thing to say. Strange, and scary.

Brahmacharya

That evening, they walked into a knot of confusion in the hostel. It was muddy football season but the boys quickly forgot all about the violence of the field. Stranger things were happening.

It had started with a puzzle. Why hadn't anybody from Room 12 gone to the dining hall for the evening snack?

The four of them were riven with confusion. Bikram Sanyal's body was the source of pain and disgust. How did the albino end up with red belt marks all over his back and waist?

He was a pale boy, as white as Europeans, with golden hair and light eyes. But he was very much homegrown. Such things happened. An illness perhaps?

He had come back early from the games today, sneaked into the bathroom for a shower. By a twist of fate, his classmate Kushal Roy returned soon enough and had also stepped into the shower. It was a dark and slippery moment, stepping into the shower with just one boy instead of the crowd back from games. But Kushal did not know that he would scream when he saw Bikram.

Welts of redness foamed across Bikram's skin and shone in the water. What were those?

Bikram had cried. It was easy to see why he wanted to shower alone. He told a story that made one cry. Two of his roommates, Asim Chatterjee, the big hairy man-boy and Nath, the football-playing Santal had tortured him for months, making him do things he couldn't bear to talk about and doing things to him that he would die before he could show anyone. For months he had taken care never to take off his shirt before another boy. And no, he could never, ever take off his pants. Never in his life before anybody. For there were things that would never go away. He cried like he was being crushed under a truck.

No one had missed Bikram at the football field because he never went to the football field in the afternoon. He was excused. He had special permission from Premen Swami, the assistant headmaster.

Premen Swami and Bikram spent every afternoon playing table-tennis in the common room of Conscience Hall, when everybody else was away at the football field.

'They did this to me for two months!' Bikram howled.

Chatterjee grabbed Bikram's collar and pulled him like a dog. 'Lying son of a whore,' he screamed. 'Your mom's tits will burn before you finish lying.'

'Swear on your heart.' Bikram said with deathly calm. 'Why do you lock our door after lights off every night?'

'Dead white goat!' Chatterjee shook the boy's collar so hard that it felt that his blonde-white head would tear from his neck. 'That's your idea! You bitch about the draft nonstop!'

'They are animals.' Bikram stared at him with dead eyes. 'The things they can do to another human being.'

Nath made a face like a monkey and stared at the boys, pointing a figure to his brain. *The wimp has lost his nuts.* They heard him loud and clear. Nath looked like a black ape and he made a grotesque face, like that of a roasting eggplant curling over a fire. He rarely spoke and he rarely needed to. *What the fuck is the albino talking about?* What language was this?

C Block was suddenly a crowded police court. Thronged by a silent mob. Everybody wanted to be there. Nobody said a word. How could you?

Someone touched Anirvan's right arm lightly. Anirvan knew who it was. He turned to his right. Kajol was shorter than him. He looked up, met Anirvan's eyes. Large, speaking eyes that had much to say.

Lightly, Anirvan squeezed his hand. There was no response.

'What is going on?' Anirvan whispered. 'How can a boy do such things to another boy? It's not like Bikram is a girl.'

Kajol frowned. He looked bitter.

Nath was still monkeying around. Some of the boys started laughing. Most were still frozen.

'I hope the monks don't come to know.' Anirvan said in a low voice. 'They would be shocked by this muck.'

'What are you saying?' Kajol whispered breathlessly. 'All of them would be thrown out of the school.'

'Don't ever say such things,' Kajol's voice shivered. 'What if they throw you out of the ashram? Then what?' Horror twitched through his body like a nerve.

'Especially Premen Swami.' Anirvan said. 'There is a

halo around him.' He was a true monk. He played with Bikram every afternoon.

Kajol frowned. Then he melted into the crowd.

Anirvan felt like slapping himself. You just didn't talk to Kajol like that. Not Kajol.

Kajol was a dream student. Never missed homework and never got under 90 per cent in any subject. He knew what mattered—Physics Chemistry Mathematics, the magic three that one needed to crack the golden gate of the top engineering colleges. With his large eyes and well-oiled hair and beautiful eyelashes, he was a source of knowledge even when he said nothing. He rarely did. But he knew the path. His shawl was supposed to trail it when he walked to memorize, the straight and simple path.

But his eyes fell on Anirvan as if sucked by gravity. It was as if his mind hovered over Anirvan no matter what he did. Soft and beautiful eyes that knew what they wanted. They wanted to own Anirvan. It turned Anirvan's heart into a soft, warm mess.

Kajol walked the path—the path of Brahmacharya— the path where one shunned electric fans and waking up late and tea and coffee and television and hardened their muscles on the jogging tracks. At the end of the road they saw the result sheets of the engineering entrance test, which is where life came to a happy ending.

The Lotus Position

Saffron sheathed Kamal Swami like skin. He was a taut bowstring, flashes of energy tossing around the smooth cotton and revealing fair, hairy flesh, patches of sweat that darkened the amber fabric as he breathed faster and faster like a stallion while Anirvan forgot to breathe, staring at muscles that shot out as saffron seawaves. His heart stopped at the glimpse of his fair and lean arm as the Swami rolled up his sleeves on the badminton court. He dreamt of owning such arms one day. These very arms.

He was a saffron soldier with the eyes of a boy, eyes that sparkled with love and mischief but which never failed to hunt down the heap of dirt the students had swept under their beds or the cricket-magazines hidden under geography textbooks. The boys' rooms were restless, with blobs of shame hidden in odd cracks like the wet towels and the used underwear they forgot to give their mothers on Sunday.

The Swami knew everything.

The boys had marched out of the common room in silence that day. After the TV was killed and they were thrown out of the stadium in Peshawar. The air was thick with war. The firecrackers had gone out in Mosulgaon but anger smoldered at the sudden death of the match.

Kamal Swami stood at the door while the boys walked out quietly, all eighty of them. His fair face looked red and stormy.

'The two of you wait here,' he said softly as Anirvan and Kajol stepped out.

They waited. They were anxious but they didn't want to look at each other.

'Those boys are a shame,' Kamal Swami told them after everybody had left. His voice throbbed with passion. 'Animals, all of them.'

Anirvan and Kajol stood in silence. They looked down, wilted in shame. They didn't know what to say.

'You boys stay away from them.'

His voice was kind. Kind but cruel.

'From now on the two of you will sit at the back of the prayer hall.' He said softly. 'I want you to watch if any boy makes trouble. Just tell me if you see anything.'

What was Kajol thinking? Suddenly, the question screamed inside Anirvan's heart.

'You will spread out our prayer mats before prayer.' The Swami said. 'And put them back after it's over.'

Every night after the lights were off the Swami sat on the wooden bench outside his room and spoke about life, death, and life beyond life. When the day was over and their duties done, his voice was softer, kinder, and sometimes almost aimless. The boys could not see his face in the dark but his affectionate hands caressed their shoulders and the backs of their necks and slid along their arms in ways they never would in daylight. It was good to sit right next to him but it was not always possible because many boys crowded the bench after lights-off. But his voice melted in the dark and floated everywhere even if you were not lucky enough to sit next to him that night. He said the most beautiful things. Once Rajeev Lochan Sen had popped a tough question about the point of studying history. It was a scrap of a debate that floated in school for days.

'Is history a dead subject?' The Swami had laughed. Under the nightly softness, the laughter had a bite, and Anirvan imagined the pointed edges of his crooked teeth glistening in the dark.

'Go and look at yourself in a mirror,' he said.

'Mirror?' Rajeev repeated, full of wonder.

Kajol had walked into the gathering tentatively. He looked like he had lost his way.

'Move over,' Kamal Swami said. 'Kajol, sit next to Anirvan.'

There was no place next to Anirvan. The slight-framed Kajol came and sat on Anirvan's lap.

'Take a hard look at yourself,' the Swami's voice softened. 'What you see in that mirror is history.'

Rajeev was lucky that night. He was seated next to the Lotus.

'This face, this neck, these shoulders,' the Swami's voice trailed in the dark. 'The messy hair and the frown. The clothes you wear.'

'You'll see all of it in the mirror, won't you?' the voice floated, suddenly happy and boyish.

'This is history,' it said. 'And you ask whether history is a living being?'

Rajeev was silent. Anirvan wondered if his doubts were gone. But Anirvan didn't care anymore; he felt lightheaded. Kajol's childlike frame rested on him, and he could smell soap and talcum powder on his neck.

Anirvan knew why the Lotus was so brilliant at carrom. He could handle his mind like the red striker on the board. Anirvan had tried it too. He thought he could do it. *Leave your mind, swim out of it, and watch it wander.* The Great Saffron One had said a hundred years ago. *Watch it like a fish bobbing in the water, a trivial thing of colour that is no longer part of you.* Anirvan could lose his mind in the prayer hall, during the meditation time at the end, at least for a minute, two minutes, two minutes and twenty seconds...

Kajol's moist eyes were a lie. Anirvan realized that Kajol knew what he wanted. Anirvan belonged to him. Kajol did not speak much but his will was sharp. He would draw Anirvan closer, tie him up, shape his days.

There were rules. He could never get Kajol to break a rule. Sometimes, Anirvan cut the games hours in the afternoons and wandered around the ashram, often hiding in the huge library. They were supposed to be on the playground. It could be nasty if someone caught them.

They spoke a lot. Kajol's words had the spiky weight of a teenager whose voice had started to crack. It was clumsy, their conversation, but they wanted to talk to each other forever so it didn't matter. Kajol wanted to savour

Anirvan's words and Anirvan wanted to draw out Kajol's heavy, faltering voice as if he was dragging a cart on a bed of stones. They sat and said meaningless things to each other. They got in each other's way much more than Anirvan had realized before—in school, the dining hall, the bathroom, on the walk to school, in the assembly line; numbed out of their minds on the way to the prayer that started school—the prayer that pleaded for them to be taken from darkness to light. There was always a sunburst of happiness whenever he saw Kajol. Kajol always smiled but he did not speak much when other boys were around. There were signs. They had a system of sign and whisper.

He wanted Kajol to cut games too. Four to six—they could wander around for two hours, play ping pong in the common room, Kajol could even help him with algebra. They could talk.

'Game time?' Kajol said in shock. 'We cannot miss games.'

'Why?' Anirvan asked. 'We can walk around the orchard behind the football ground. No one ever goes there.'

'It's against the rules,' was all Kajol would say. 'Bad idea.'

He would never do it.

Quietly, he looked away, making sure their eyes did not meet.

So Anirvan wandered around alone, sometimes staying back in his room with scattered schoolwork all around so if a monk or a teacher caught him he could say he was studying. A few days later, while he was rearranging things in his desk, Kajol walked into his room.

It was 5.30 and the boys usually came back to the hostel a few minutes before 6 and then the shower room became a muddy screaming match. But at 5.30, the hostel was quiet and empty. The teachers usually went out at this time and the monks...no one knew where the monks went.

It was football season and Kajol wore an Argentinian jersey that was plastered to his body. He was sweaty but very little dirt had touched him. He played just enough but never so wildly as to get really dirty.

'You're back already?' Anirvan asked.

'Yes,' Kajol said. 'Thought I'd see what you were up to.'

Happiness was a warm flood in Anirvan's chest.

They were not sure what to talk about.

'I'll go and shower,' Kajol said.

'I'll come too,' Anirvan said.

Each hostel block had a large bathroom with a row of toilet stalls and a large shower area with five showers. Shower times, morning and evening, were a mayhem of shrieks and screams and water games and spray violence with sixteen boys from four rooms jostling for the five showers, taking turns and sometimes wrestling under the rain.

It felt huge with just the two of them in there. Football season was monsoon season, and the days were long and shiny.

They were both in their shorts. Anirvan loved looking at Kajol's body. It was small and dark and slim, but nicely shaped with small, billowing muscles as he never missed a PT or games session and always threw himself wholeheartedly into the madness of rules. His collarbones were shiny and afloat.

Anirvan felt a slight shame standing in front of him without his shirt. He was also thin but his body was uneven, lacking the sportsman's billowy shape. He was bigger than Kajol and felt clumsy.

Quickly, he ran the shower and closed his eyes. Water, warm from the sunbaked water tanks on the terrace, washed over his body.

He didn't know how long he had kept his eyes closed. Perhaps ten seconds, perhaps fifteen. He heard Kajol's voice through the spray of water.

'How do you meditate?' He asked. 'How do you empty your mind?'

Anirvan was quiet. He wanted to say something but he couldn't speak.

'I just can't do it,' Kajol said. 'Whenever I try to do it, thoughts crowd my head.'

Anirvan wanted to open his eyes. But the spray of water made it impossible.

He tilted his head, popping out of the halo of water.

'I didn't know you wanted to meditate.' He said.

'It cleans your mind,' Kajol said. 'Helps with math.'

Anirvan closed his eyes again.

'They say if you stare at something real hard,' Kajol said, 'everything around it vanishes.'

Anirvan stared at the knob that turned the shower. He stared hard, not talking, and after a while Anirvan started feeling a bit sleepy but everything was still there. The rain. The liver-coloured wall of the bathroom. Kajol's

red towel hung over it. Kajol was there too; Anirvan stole
a glance at him, the bony ribcage rising and falling with
his breath. Water ran over his soft brown skin; it was as
if he was swimming underwater.

He opened his eyes. Kajol was staring at him. He was
Kajol's thing.

'You breathe long and hard.' Kajol said. 'Your ribs
stick out sharp.'

'One, two, three, four,' he touched and counted them.
Suddenly, Anirvan started breathing faster. He wished he
could breathe as if meditating because that drew out his
ribs sharp and clear.

Kajol traced his ribs like a child who had just learned
counting. His fingers lingered on Anirvan's belly-button;
slowly, his index finger dug inside.

All the life left in Anirvan was in his belly-button—the
centre of his body, where the serpent lay in sleep. Would
the serpent wake up?

Anirvan could not stare things away. But he could
step back and watch his body breathe. Slowly, he could
disown his body. There it was, breathing away. There was
nothing else.

He could never be like Kamal Swami.

But slowly, Anirvan could float out of his body. Soon,
he just watched it breathe and get wet under the shower.
It wasn't his body any longer. It pumped itself like a brute
animal. Anirvan swam away from it, like a wisp of incense
smoke in the prayer hall.

Slowly, he opened his eyes. Before him was Kajol's
right collarbone. Under the water, it shone like a knife.

'Yogi!'

Kajol laughed his little-boy laughter.

'You're just gone!' He said. 'You can really tune out. Like a real Yogi!'

Kajol's voice shivered.

A Yogi. One who could cane and whip his mind into a sharp and shiny machine.

Don't fight it. The Lotus said.

Slip out of it like you slip out of your shirt. Watch it play, a cheap toy. Slowly, the mind will become your slave.

The Lotus, he knew, could do anything. He could be like Arjun. Arjun shut out the rest of the world, fixed his gaze on the wooden bird on the tree, and shot its head off with his arrow. The carrom striker became an arrow in Kamal Swami's fingers. The red monster shot at the circle of coins at the heart of the board and ripped it open, sending a cluster of the right coins to the pocket. It was like a blast of dynamite.

Anirvan felt terrified to see the explosive force stored in the smooth, saffron-robed monk. But if you controlled your mind you controlled the striker. Kamal Swami, he knew, could stare hard at a coin so as to make everything else vanish from his vision. And then destroy it. Kamal Swami. The Lord Lotus.

Meditation was a skill crucial to life in the ashram. It sharpened your mind, helped you master algebra, geometry and physics. Everything one needed to crack the engineering entrance tests. The boys stared at the tests, five years down the line, and tried to make the rest of the world vanish. How do you think the ancient Indians invented the zero and other foundations of mathematics? Kajol always said. And he cracked the puzzles of geometry so smoothly that it seemed that he felt the problems and the answers like tremors in his own body. *His lovely bony body.*

How do you think? Because yoga is the foundation of mathematics.

Yogi. Kajol fell in a kind of a spell whenever Anirvan meditated under the shower. Sometimes when Anirvan's mind wavered, he could feel Kajol's liquid stare on his skin. Sometimes Kajol would touch him lightly and Anirvan's focus would shatter. *Yogi.* Kajol called him Yogi. The one who has mastered Yoga. One who controls his mind like a steel toy. It became his name. No one remembered Anirvan.

But Yogi would never be like the Lotus. Could he?

Suddenly, without warning, the Swami could become softer, gentler. That's what happened during the Diwali mini-vacation that year.

They had only four days off around Diwali so a few students stayed back at the hostel. Mostly the boys who lived far away, and the poor village and tribal boys who didn't always want to go home as life was much better in the ashram. Anirvan stayed back too. It was never difficult to convince his parents why he should spend more and more time away from home. Anirvan told Kajol that morning that he was not going home and Kajol had said nothing.

'I'm staying back too,' he told Anirvan in the dining hall that evening. Anirvan felt struck with a lightning of delight. *Yes!*

There were no rules during these few days. Only three other boys had stayed back in Bliss Hall, sporty tribal boys who played football all day. There was no morning bell, no PT, no prayer, no study hall, and no school. The whole day was theirs. They could do whatever they wanted.

They spent the entire morning playing carrom with Kamal Swami. The Lotus was softer, intimate; his voice sounded different. He cracked jokes while striking the carrom disks on the board. What a player! When he aimed the striker, his soul was focused on the board. Like there was nothing else in the world. He never lost a match.

When they went to take a shower, Anirvan and Kajol were the only ones in the hostel. The bathroom felt big and hollow. It echoed every word they uttered. So they showered in silence, next to each other, playing games, laughing quietly. Kajol clamped the mouth of the faucet and shot a blinding water jet at Anirvan. He drowned Anirvan in water and laughter. There was nothing else in the world. The bathroom door was open and yet no one would ever come; they could take as long as they wanted.

Kajol was another boy. Free, wild, noisy. His still eyes sparkled. He wouldn't take his eyes off Anirvan. The campus was empty and the place didn't feel like a school anymore. It was a sandy saffron place of happiness.

After lunch, they wandered around the ashram. They walked all over the endless campus, spread over eighty villages from the past. No one stopped them anywhere.

When school was on, they were not allowed to leave the limits of the junior school. But today they walked from the junior school through the winding lanes crowded by mango trees to the senior school. They wandered past the stadium into the senior school, where the hostels and the buildings seemed larger, shinier. Everything was empty. Everybody had vanished and there was no outside world and no time ticking along. But Kajol seemed to belong to the ashram, a plant nourished by its sun and soil.

The campus was a place of play. They lost their way and walked into the school for the disabled boys but nobody shouted at them. The people smiled and led them back to the route to the junior school. On the way back, they flung stones at the mango trees to bring down mangoes but nothing happened; mango season was long over. Their palms twirled against one another and stayed there as they walked. They laughed and joked and tried not to notice it. They drifted apart as they stepped back into the junior school campus.

In the evening they went back to Kamal Swami's room. The room looked dark but as they peeped through the door, they saw a blue light.

A night lamp was on and the Swami was seated on the floor in the lotus position. He opened his eyes as he heard them at the door. He gestured, calling them inside.

The Swami sat in a narrow space between his bed and the wall. Kajol went and sat behind him on the floor. Anirvan sat at the end, behind Kajol.

The Swami closed his eyes and went back into meditation.

The small room looked ghostly in that blue light. Grey cotton things hung from the bedstead and the furniture cast long shadows. The windows were shut. The smell of incense danced like a raincloud and the air felt cool. Anirvan reached out and encircled Kajol's waist with his arms.

They straightened their spines and sat in the padmasana—the Lotus seat. They closed their eyes. In a daze, Anirvan slid his fingers down and felt the heat of Kajol's hardened penis. He felt safe, and at peace.

They heard the sound of the wall clock. Tick, tock. Tick, tock.

And then the sound melted away.

Dinner was like a picnic. The three football players were back. The exhausting daylong game had made them more talkative and they cracked jokes that were lost to those who had stayed away from the field. But nobody felt left out and it was like a little festival in the dining hall, which only had seven people in it—the five boys, Kamal Swami and the caretaker Nitai who was a villager from the deep interior of rural Bengal.

'Luben kicks like a demon on the field,' Nitai said.

Luben Kisku ate silently but a smile had crept into his face. He was one of the tribal boys who rarely spoke. But he was the magical athlete whom everybody loved.

'Was shooting the ball like a bullet and all I could do was to duck at the goal.' Nitai laughed.

'The lungiwallah from Mosulgaon was playing the goalie behind the goalpost,' Naren Das said. 'He caught the ball every time and kicked it back to us.'

Naren Das was a poor village boy who was a math geek and a deadly football stopper. He had a tiny face but spoke like a sage.

'The men from Mosulgaon were there?' Kamal Swami asked calmly.

'Oh yes,' Nitai said. And then suddenly his voice fell to a whisper. 'They always slip into the stadium when the boys play.'

Anirvan and Kajol listened to them but said nothing. Kajol was a good football player but today he hadn't gone to the fields at all. There were no rules today.

Their voices rose to a crescendo. The Lotus smiled and cracked jokes. The boys looked up in wonder.

'Luben smiles like a sweet little girl,' the Swami said. 'And on the field he shoots the ball like lightning to split your guts open.'

Everybody laughed. Luben kept smiling but said nothing.

'But he doesn't pass the ball,' Sanket Tudu, another tribal boy, said gloomily. 'He wants to play alone.'

'Arre who cares!' Nitai said. 'He shoots so well, he can tear apart any net. Today I thought he would kill the Mosulgaon bastards behind the goalpost.'

'My blood had started to boil,' he went on. 'Took me back to those days when there was nothing but forests here—forests and savage villages where these people wandered around.'

Nitai went on. Suddenly the old man had slipped back forty years in the past.

'We came in with sticks and spears and chased the

split-dicks out of their homes.' He looked dreamy. 'And
only then they could put up the walls of the ashram.'

'Nitai,' Kamal Swami said sharply.

Nitai froze.

Yogi looked at Kamal Swami's face and his heart
stopped. The Swami's face had darkened.

Silence sat there for several long seconds.

'Hey,' the Lotus smiled. 'Get a couple of more eggs for
Luben. I bet he can eat a village today.'

Everybody laughed.

They walked down the long corridor that joined the
dining hall to the blocks that housed their rooms. The
football players had wandered off again, and Nitai was
nowhere to be seen. Kamal Swami walked with Anirvan
and Kajol.

Jackals howled in the distance. They sounded faraway
but they were closer. The boys had heard the stories. How
they used to slither across the campus just ten years ago.
The ashram had been built on wild, savage villages. The
past was fearful.

The Lotus walked slowly. His feet, covered with thick
socks, made no noise. He walked up the stairs. Anirvan
and Kajol followed him. His saffron robe looked darker
in the night, almost mournful.

They paused before Kajol's room.

'Why don't you stay here tonight?' The Lotus looked
at Anirvan. 'You'll be scared to sleep alone, won't you?'

Anirvan's heart jumped with joy. Quickly, he looked
at Kajol. Kajol's face was flooded with the slippery light
of happiness.

'I'll get my things,' Anirvan said quickly, as if he was afraid the Swami would change his mind.

'Before you go to sleep,' Kamal Swami said, 'close your eyes and cleanse your mind.'

'Yoga works best when you do it with a partner,' he said. 'But you must learn to hold your essence. Breathe deep and cultivate self-control.'

He vanished across the corridor.

The Lord of Love

There were things in Anirvan's life that had to be hidden from Sushant Kane. That made him feel shameful and a little criminal. SrK meant something real. He gave colour to the world.

He had never seen SrK and Kamal Swami speak to each other.

SrK would never know that the Swami gave Anirvan special duties. Never. But Anirvan had to talk to SrK.

'It's strange,' Anirvan said. 'My mind feels lost when they turn the lights off after prayer.'

SrK nodded. The two of them walked towards Conscience Hall.

'It's like I've lost the power to think,' Anirvan said.

'Happens,' SrK said. 'The slow music. The smell of incense. The flowers.'

'It's so beautiful,' Anirvan whispered.

'It's beautiful,' SrK said. 'It's not life.'

Anirvan was quiet.

'The monks say the world is Maya.' SrK said softly. 'It's not the world; they have Maya here. The incense and the flowers and the music.'

'The three of us came here as orphans,' he said. 'Almost as orphans…well, never mind that.

'Prashant and Ashant lived their lives in the football field. Ever since they were little boys. The monks loved that. They like to say you can get closer to god by playing football than by reading the Gita. They came back from the football field, showered, and fell into the prayer hall. The music, the incense, and the flowers.'

They walked through the darkness. Distant light fell on the yellow hostel buildings to their right, their manicured gardens shaped like different letters of the alphabet.

'They could never leave it,' SrK's voice softened. 'And so it has been for thirty years. The football ground, the gymnasium, cadet training and the prayer hall. The sweat of the boys and the saffron robes.'

'But you are here too.' A bright spark caught Anirvan's voice as he spoke.

'Yes, I stayed on as a teacher,' SrK said. 'The boys love us.'

'But,' he turned to Anirvan with a smile. 'I don't like the smell of incense.'

That was easy to tell. He smelled of cigarettes.

'Tell me,' suddenly he turned to Anirvan. 'Why do you like it when they turn off the lights after prayer?'

'It feels so beautiful and quiet,' Anirvan said eagerly. 'Like the world is covered in silence.'

'And what's so great about silence?' Smiling, SrK looked at him. 'A debater loves the chatter of words!'

But he does. SrK had sensed something in him. Something he couldn't name himself. But he was right. Words have power. They can kill. Maybe someday he would be an orator. Or a writer of fiery pamphlets.

Something crazy and powerful. Would he? Perhaps, maybe. The annual debating competition was coming closer. They were getting ready. They would go and rehearse in Conscience Hall, the hostel where the boys of Class 9 lived.

Yogi didn't feel like talking.

Rajeev Lochan Sen, singer and debater, joined them as they approached Conscience Hall. Walking through the fragrant darkness of the ashram, Rajeev became his usual flowing self, singing an old Hindi song. He had a beautiful voice, a bit melodramatic at times, but beautiful. He liked to touch people while singing, gesturing them to join in the song. Anirvan smiled clumsily as he had no music in him, none at all. But he listened.

This was an unusual evening, given away entirely to debate practice. Anirvan was happy; Kajol, too, was here today. Kajol didn't care much for debates and extracurriculars but Anirvan had made him come. Kajol did not like to budge from his habits of spending time, most of which revolved around his studies. Sometimes Anirvan pulled and pushed him in different directions, keen to see how far he would stretch for him. Kajol came sometime, always whining about it.

Sushant Kane had a strange way of training them. Suddenly he was like his brothers on the sports field. His dead face watched the boys spew memorized lines. His mouth winced and shrieked, 'Hold it!' To proceed to take apart the last sentence spewed, toss and turn the verb around, repeat the sentence in such a way so as to twist its nature crooked. Most of the time he stared at the ceiling. The senior boys also found him strange. Most of the time he was laughable but suddenly he had spiky, poisonous edges.

They did not take words seriously enough. They did not pause over them long enough. They did not think or wonder. A few boys poured out speeches their parents had written for them, in a kind of electric manner acquired over home-made dishes during the visiting hours. They were ridged with Sanskrit and listening to them one felt the British were still ruling India and everybody was throbbing with virtuous anger. Anirvan's parents knew nothing of his debating activities. But he also loved big words and piled them high in his speech—because he could! He rushed through them like a sprinter tackling rocky, mountainous terrain, flying but never faltering. Sushant Kane tripped him up. He threw many of the rocks and cliffs away and tried to make him walk on level ground. It made Yogi unhappy. SrK didn't think he could manage the difficult words.

Anirvan had to make him understand.

'A speech is simply a conversation with many people at the same time,' SrK said. 'A conversation where you are the only one talking.' He looked around the room. 'But a conversation.'

He looked at the debaters who were actually anti-British rebels simmering in anger. 'And a speech is not war either. Relax.'

'You know the saying—the candied knife. Smile sweetly and stab,' his face was expressionless as he spoke. 'Look like the Buddha while silently pulling their arteries apart.'

Words were Anirvan's friends. He had a way with them. SrK always said. He had such a way of saying it, it gave Anirvan gooseflesh every time he did. He wanted Anirvan to go with it. Where did he want him to go? Anirvan groped and tried to reach for it but couldn't. And SrK wouldn't tell him.

For SrK, words were supernatural.

The boys with home-cooked speeches didn't know what to say. Their breath still smelled of mom-made chicken kosha.

'But it's…it's…' a boy of class eight stammered. 'It's about s…saving the nation.'

'And why's it about saving the nation?' Sushant Kane frowned, looking impatient for the first time. 'Why isn't it about a bat flying against the moon at night?'

A chill ran through their bodies. Everybody stared at him. There he was, with his bats and goats and lightning and lamp-posts.

'But, Sushant-da,' Shome said. 'The subject is whether studies are nirvana for students. Or they should break the walls of the classroom and work for the poor nation.'

The theme was a perverse rephrasing of a statement by an anti-British nationalist who became a friend of Hitler, who had asked young people for their blood so that he could give them freedom. It was the kind of theme, they knew, that made Sushant Kane lose his cool.

The monks chose the themes of the annual debates. They usually went well with the breathless rocky terrain style sprinting and naturally demanded large, musical words.

'Does that mean you have to make a speech about it?' Sushant Kane frowned. 'Why can't you have a chat?'

The senior boys stared at one another. *Here we go again!*

Sushant Kane had a reputation. He cheapened serious things. He was allergic to the smooth glow of saffron.

Rajeev was about to say something when they heard the noise outside. Like the muffled sound of a bomb. And then there was another, and the noise of a table crashing.

'Premen Swami,' one of the senior boys murmured, his face pale as death. Love Swami, the Love Lord.

They stepped out of the common room but stood frozen at the door. It was Niroj Bora, the reckless boy from Guwahati who always hurried into trouble, full of revenge against rules. He was a big, muscular boy but the giant figure of Premen Swami tossed him around like a dry twig in a storm. He pulled him by his hair and hit him in a blinding flurry of flying saffron robes and the bomb went off again; Bora shot to the other end of the hallway. The Love Lord sped after him, a miraculous 100+ kg mass of saffron and a pale, shaved head, lifted up the crumpled boy and banged his fist on him again—back, shoulders, cheeks; it came like rain. The carrom board perched at the end of the hallway had crashed and the wooden pillars that had held it up lay scattered on the floor.

The Love Lord breathed like a massive mute animal

as he threw Bora around. It was a phlegmatic groan, as if he had a lung disease. Parts of his monastic robe had darkened with sweat. His face, beaded with perspiration, was strangely blank, as if his hands were wreaking the violence on their own and he had nothing to do with it. Bora was a tough nut to crack. He did not utter a word or say sorry, and nobody could imagine him cry. He grimaced, dodging a blow or two, but he knew better than to try to defend himself. Blocking a blow would unleash a whole new river of fury. Nobody wanted to see it. Bora's head might be smashed against the wall, bloodying the plaster with a giant red stain.

Nobody said a word. It was a private chat between The Love Lord and Bora. A wordless chat where each understood the other. The Love Lord was notorious for his spells of violence, but he always chose the same kind—the toughest and the most dangerous kind of boy, those with bones and nerves hard enough to take the killer spasm of blows. Usually they were the ones who kicked Mission rules out of their way. What was it this time?

Sushant Kane stood with a grimace on his face.

'The ping-pong tournament,' someone whispered.

'What about the ping-pong tournament?' Rajeev asked.

'The ping-pong tournament,' the senior boy whispered breathlessly, eyes rapt in terror.

The Love Lord pulled Bora by his collar. The thin cotton shirt ripped apart, baring Bora's dark brown skin. The monk's splayed palm exploded on the flesh. It made a sharper, naked kind of a bang. Had he been pale-skinned it would have left red hand prints on his back, but Bora was tough and brown, his skin the colour of the muddied football fields during the monsoon. The raging monk tore the collar apart and Bora's strong neck flew out proudly. Suddenly, the Love Lord tasted blood; his blows now brought the sharp, stinging noise of flesh on flesh. His palms, they knew, were soft and pale and doughy; to boys who knew, its power was a shock. Bora's shirt buttons popped out in fury and were flung all over the hallway. Half-naked, he stared defiantly at the glassy-eyed monk. A sharp slap sent him flying to the other end of the balcony and his face crashed against the steel mullions that looked out to the lawns.

The monk beckoned Bora with his ring-studded fingers. Bora collected his crumpled self and stood up, still unbroken.

The Swami held out a key.

'Go to my room,' he stared at the boy with lifeless eyes. 'And bring my rod.'

Anirvan stepped back into the common room. He didn't want to see the next scene. Never.

The thud they heard a few minutes later chilled their spines. It was as if a heavy blanket had muffled the violence and it couldn't breathe. Like iron fillings drawn to a magnet, they crowded the door again.

Bora stood holding the mullions on the balcony facing the lawn. He was shirtless.

The Love Lord struck him with the cane. Bora shook as if electrocuted.

And then he screamed.

The cane lashed at his legs. Would the Love Lord break his knees?

Bora cried, a wet and terrifying moan.

'Premen,' a voice thundered from the end of the corridor.

Kamal Swami stood there, a looming saffron tower.

The Love Lord froze.

He wiped his face on his sleeves, looked at Bora like he wanted to spit on him. Then he stormed away.

The Lotus walked up to Bora. He picked up his t-shirt from the floor.

'Here,' he said. 'Put it on.'

Bora burst into tears. Suddenly, everything shattered inside Anirvan. The massive brute animal.

The Lotus ruffled his hair playfully.

'What have you done now?' He asked, smiling.

'We rigged the tournament,' Bora burst out between his tears. 'It was supposed to be a lottery. I'll never do it again. Never.' He sobbed. 'I promise.'

Gently, Kamal Swami caressed his back. Bora screamed. His back was on fire.

The Lotus stepped away.

'Go and say "sorry" to Premen,' he said softly. 'You know he loves you. That is why he gets so mad.'

'Go,' he whispered.

The boys breathed.

Anirvan realized his hand was tightly clenched around Kajol's. Kajol, too, held him in a squeeze. Their palms were wet with sweat.

Sushant Kane seemed to chew his food forever. His face was clouded, and he stared at the wall before him. The old, perfumed chemistry teacher Himesh Lahiri smiled and said something. But Sushant Kane did not reply. He kept his gaze on the wall and kept chewing. There couldn't possibly be any food left in his mouth; he must have been chewing his own teeth. He seemed to eat very little, lesser even than what he usually ate.

Premen Swami sat at the hostel warden's place. He took two places, he was so big. And so tall, he could see all the way to the end of the dining hall even while seated. In Conscience Hall, the dining hall was quiet and well-behaved and the trouble boys never cared where they sat. Even in the rows farthest away from the staff tables, they were under The Love Lord's eyes. No one knew what might happen if somebody made a mistake.

Today the staff table looked different. Mihir Dam was there as usual. He was a short and squat elderly man who taught PT and football to the senior boys. But next to him sat Niroj Bora, with a dinner that didn't look like it belonged to the ashram. It was designed on special orders from the Love Lord. A pair of juicy chicken drumsticks stuck out from a bowl of golden sauce and next to it was another bowl with the massive head of a fish. Even on chicken nights all the boys got were three measly pieces and could not even dream of such glorious drumsticks. It was an unreal kind of a spread and the bowl of creamy, soft rosomalai that sat at the end of the semi-circle of bowls was not part of any meal the boys had ever seen at the ashram—dessert rarely reached their tables.

Bora was absorbed in his dinner. He had showered and put on new clothes. His moist hair was combed neatly and slicked over his head. He did not look up from his plate.

His leg was serrated with long black marks. Everybody knew. The Love Lord's wooden cane had a metal wire entwined around it.

'It's good to see this boy eat, isn't it?' Mihir Dam, the senior PT teacher said as he cleared a wisp of chicken from between his teeth. 'Boys these days have chicken-stomachs! When we were boys—that was a whole other matter!'

'When we were boys, the custom was to fatten the calf before slaughtering it.' Sushant Kane said without looking up from his food. 'These days the calf is fattened *after* slaughter.'

'What?' Mihir Dam stopped chewing. A frown appeared on his face.

The Love Lord lifted his face. Glassy eyes stared at Sushant Kane.

Sushant Kane walked back to Bliss Hall after dinner, with Anirvan, Rajeev and Kajol. It was a still and humid night. There was no shiver in the leaves. Yet there was something lovely about the open air of the ashram. To be out in the night was beautiful.

They walked in silence. Rajeev hummed a tune softly, a Tagore song popular in their music classes. They slowed down, in no hurry to reach Bliss Hall.

'How do you fatten a calf *after* slaughter?' Anirvan asked.

Sushant Kane said nothing. He stared ahead in the semi darkness of the road. Rajeev looked at Anirvan and smiled, still humming the tune.

'With chicken and fish and rosomalai!' Kane said. His voice was matter-of-fact and he still wouldn't look at them.

Suddenly, a chill ran along Anirvan's skin. He remembered the thud of Bora's face against the steel mullions of the hallway.

'Mihir Da was totally lost.' Rajeev stopped humming and said. 'He was looking around for calves.'

'You said it,' Anirvan stumbled, 'in...in such a way.' With such a dead sort of peace, he wanted to say.

'Do you think Premen Swami understood?' Rajeev asked in his shrill, musical voice.

'Calves.' Sushant Kane said to the darkness. 'Calves for pleasure and violence.'

That was how it went. Premen Swami saw nothing but the boy for days. The boy he chose, casting his killer eye on him, watching every mistake. One day he would call him aside, whisper darkly, tell him that he was going to fall off the cliff. And then the day would come like a curse and the Love Lord would rip open his flesh, savouring its soft tearable brownness, bruising his bare back and thighs, running loving fingers across the cane-bites across his shoulders. They were tangled in a raw mess from which none could free them. The tangle would end at dinner when the bruised boy was fed the feast of princes and he would eat, happy and grateful, for the red welts on his skin and the extra pair of chicken drumsticks in his bowl. That was how it went.

Premen Swami had attacked Nath, the athletic tribal, just a few days back as if he was going to break him into small blood-stained pieces. Right after the soft-skinned albino Bikram Sanyal had complained to him about Nath and Chatterjee and their dance of shame around the red belt marks on his white skin. Bikram had cried and cried the whole time the Swami had tossed and turned Nath around, the brutal tribal who had refused to cry or beg for mercy. Neither would the bullied shame leave Bikram easy. He had spent the night in the Love Lord's room where the Swami had consoled him all night.

Nobody would ever dare say anything about the marks on his body again.

How did the Love Lord fatten the calf after slaughter? How did he do it?

'Is that why you ask us to tone down the drama in our speeches?' Rajeev asked. 'Cut the rocky road-stormy ocean style?'

'We live in the age of cinema,' Sushant Kane said. 'And you guys shout like it's a medieval folk play on the village grounds.'

'The candied knife.' Rajeev said, trancelike.

'Look around for calves?' Sushant Kane said, his voice down to a whisper. 'Mihir Dam was not looking around for calves. Calves for slaughter. Everyone knows what that means.'

There was a chill in the air.

'Everyone knows why he rips them up,' SrK said, dreamlike. 'Flowers, incense, music, the nasha. They beat them up because they want to do something else they can't.' He whispered. 'Not always.'

The chill caressed Anirvan. Did everybody know what the Love Lord did to his calves? How he licked and clawed and cut them open and then soothed them with a prince's spread at night?

'I was four when I was brought to the ashram. Prashant was seven, and Ashant was just two. Prashant and I only spoke Marathi, Ashant spoke nothing. The monks taught us Bengali.' He paused. 'It's a trickster's language.'

What is a trickster's language? What did one do to fatten one's calves after slaughter?

A pang of desire shot through Anirvan. Would he learn to trick with language? Grip and thrall them without looking like he was trying?

A *trickster's language?* He felt confused.

They had arrived at the steps of Bliss Hall. Kajol freed his hand from Anirvan.

'Premen Swami wasn't tricked.' Kajol said, suddenly.

Sushant Kane paused at the steps. He looked at them. 'Stay sharp. They can kill you. You won't know you're dead.'

They stepped into Bliss Hall.

The King Who Owned Nothing

Anirvan's father helped his grandmother to her death. Happily. He was that kind of a man.

The doctor looked grim the day they took her away to the hospital. But Anirvan's father looked joyful, wearing his bloated white pajamas as if he had forgotten that he would have to change and step out of home, go with his mother to the hospital in a condition the doctor said only 1 per cent of people survived.

Anirvan's grandmother was in a joking mood. The whole time. Her body had melted into the coarse cotton of the hospital bed. Something about her was like a little girl, ribs poking and all. She would quickly become popular in the ward of the hospital where she lay, laughing and singing songs. Anirvan saw her laughing whenever he went for a visit. Her body was shrunken, little-girlish. He never fully understood what was wrong with her, just that something was sick with her inner organs. She had lost most of her weight and her white cotton sari flapped on the bed.

There was a young woman on a bed next to her, almost a girl. She was probably eighteen or nineteen, dark, thin, and pretty. Anirvan had started to like her. She was one of those people who are so good-natured to be always happy, but in a shy way. She had become good friends with his grandmother, which was why he liked her so much.

'Mashima sings songs for me.' The girl told him. He never asked her name. She called his grandmother mashima—auntie—which sounded strange as his grandmother was too old to be her aunt. But she said it naturally, and spoke as if his grandmother was her friend. She spoke softly, and talked about his grandmother's singing as if it were a gift given to her.

Anirvan realized that his grandmother would never come back home. The ward was not of this world. The girl was going to die too. She was so young, and so happy there, such good friends with his grandmother, who seemed to notice nothing, just laugh and sing and make her neighbours happy. It was all beautiful and magical and absurd and his heart weighed like a stone every time he walked out of the ward at the end of the visiting hour.

His father didn't care about his grandmother. Things would be simpler if she died. Anirvan's aunts, doting daughters of his grandmother softly complained that he did not look after their mother. He spent most of his time with Ivy Kar, the dark and ugly typist from his office. She had cast a spell on him. He was gravitating towards the dirty world of rustic refugees. Why did he want to marry her?

To become man and wife was to start a lifelong fight. Marriage was a violent thing.

People cried about his father and said many things.

'Which member of our family has ever stayed in a

government hospital?' They cried. 'And that too in a ward with so many people?'

'Couldn't Tushar pay for a private cabin?'

Everybody knew he was drawing money from the old woman's account, the little money left over from the dissolution of her husband's estate.

But Anirvan already knew his father did not care if his mother was alive or dead. With a slight preference towards the dead.

He knew it that night when she bled in the dark.

She had stepped out to go to the bathroom in the little balcony outside her room. Anirvan's father refused to keep a night nurse. They were expensive. So she had to get up on her own even though it took her a long time to walk just a few feet. Anirvan slept in her room, on the empty bed of his grandfather. He woke up when he heard the metallic clang of the tin mug on the balcony like a piercing cry. He rushed out onto the balcony to see his grandmother sprawled on the floor. Blood gushed from her head, a black stream in the moonlight. She was quiet. When she saw him, she asked him to help her in her usual soft voice.

It meant nothing to his father and things went on as before. But the blackness of the blood gleamed before his eyes and he knew his father didn't care if she was dead.

Home was a different place when his grandmother was there. It was another house. Anirvan had a special job.

He had to put his grandmother's little god, Gopal, to sleep every night, lay him down on his tiny brass bed in the shrine and draw the embroidered blanket over him; wake him up in the morning, sit him up on his tiny golden throne and place the sweets before him so that he could bless them and turn them into prasad.

The old woman gave out sunlight, where Anirvan was safe from the darkness of his father. A pale, soft and buttery man who wore flapping pajamas and chain-smoked filter-less Charminar cigarettes, a man who had made them all unhappy with his love for Ivy Kar, the young secretary in his office. Anirvan's mother refused to talk to him anymore, the proud woman who now spent most of her time in the college where she taught English. Anirvan's grandmother fought a strange kind of pride, that of high-born women when their men had women outside home; it let her face the fear of a family breaking apart.

She lived as though nothing had happened, never said a word about any of the family fights and sorrows, just drew Anirvan into the sunlight of her stories and the lust for nirvana, freedom from the cycle of birth and death and the sweat and pain of life.

For Anirvan was terrified of smells that came from his father's room, the coarse air of cigarettes and unwashed clothes, the loose pajamas that covered his soft, buttery legs. He heard people say that his father was going to leave his mother and marry Ivy Kar, the secretary who was dark and ugly and spoke in the savage East Bengal dialect.

Anirvan rarely saw his mother these days. She was a clever woman who came from a family of brilliant people

and she was sick of Anirvan's father and his woman and
the sins of rich old families who had riches no more,
nothing at all but their laziness and their love for sin.

'I fell for your father's honeyed words,' she would say
in tearful rage. 'But the men in this family are shiny pink
fruits that are rotten inside.'

'What?' His father would laugh dreamily. Ever since
Anirvan could remember, he barely noticed his mother.

'You're sick,' she would say. 'And so is your blood.'

Naturally, she hated Anirvan too for being a son of
that family, a boy who carried the seeds of sin and would
sprout them in time.

Sushant Kane smoked the same kind of cigarettes. In
the cool dark of his room, Anirvan knew, he wore the
same kind of pajamas. Anirvan stood outside his room
for so long, every day, sensing the rare whir of the electric
fan inside, catching the glimpse of pajamas that were not
allowed in the ashram.

SrK made him feel special. But he didn't make him
feel safe.

Anirvan had no idea how he got back to the Mission.
Somebody must have brought him back, perhaps his
mother as he had been loaned out just to see his sick
grandmother. And then suddenly he was back in his room,
number 22, Block V and it was a Wednesday evening and
there was a monthly exam next week.

It was past twilight and the darkness had started to

clamp around the balcony of Bliss Hall. He had never realized the foreign nature of this hour. Play time was over and everybody was back in the hostel and gathered in the dining hall where the evening tiffin was being served. They rarely came back to their rooms at this time, preferring to knot in the common room and the lawn downstairs till it was time for prayer.

He was not hungry and so he didn't go down to the dining hall. He felt numb. There was a coating of something around him, and the happy face of the girl in the hospital floated before him. She smiled in a weak, ghastly light and said, 'She sings for me.' Her face was yellow and kept withering away and the voice echoed. 'She sings for me.' And then his grandmother's laughter crackled in the background and it was a little-girl laughter and he knew she was going to die, and the girl would die also. They would all die, that entire ward where everybody was happy and friends with each other and sang songs and giggled like children. They were happy in such a place of illness because they were already dead, dead and gone and were really just a memory.

His grandmother had left him. He missed the soft white cotton of her sari and the bunch of rusted keys she kept tied to her anchal, keys which opened nothing, her softly moving, paan-chewing jaws. All would become nothing. Her stories were the air that he breathed. She was his place in the world. He was falling. There was no one to hold him.

The sobbing came as a relief. It broke through the strange coating around him and started breathing in the evening air. He cried like a wounded animal.

He stood next to Anirvan, the quiet shadow of a tree. Anirvan hadn't noticed when he had walked in. He stood at the door of their room. The monks never entered their rooms. They were too dirty for them to enter, even when they were clean, because young boys could never be clean. They stood, saffron shadows at the door, and glanced from one end to another, preying on unwashed socks rolled into balls and thrust under the beds and muddied school shoes. They never stepped in but cleaned everything with their glance.

'Grandmother make you sad?' Kamal Swami's voice was so gentle.

The sobs quaked through him.

He knew about his grandmother. He had given permission for Anirvan to go home in the middle of the week. *The boy will never see her again.* They had said. He had let him go.

The words flooded through him. 'She's going to go.' He said. 'Soon. She sings and laughs in the hospital. My father wants her dead. She fell down and hit her head on the railings and the balcony was full of blood and he never came out to see her. There was so much blood.'

He could not stop. He went back to the past, dug at it, slithered inside like a burrowed animal, flung back clumps and clumps of earthen past at the kind, soft-voiced man in saffron who was his only shelter. The early evening light shone on his green, shaven cheeks and the purity and the beauty of his body gave him gooseflesh. He wanted this form. He wanted this form to be his. He would tell him everything. That his mother did not speak to his father any more. Even she was appalled by the way he treated Anirvan's grandmother. But now she was going to die and there would be no one left for him.

Saffron was the colour of magic. A magic that deepened with the evening. He stood there, and his fevered chatter slithered into him like homing birds returning to their nest. They were no more. The evening was quiet as if there had been no words.

'Cry well.' He said. 'Cry. Fill your heart with tears and blow it all out.'

And he cried. He cried to him. He spoke to him through the tears and he spoke better than when he had used words.

Anirvan floated again. He was lighter, much lighter. The Swami's saffron robes smelled clean and fresh, the clean fragrance of cotton. He stood away from Anirvan and yet the peace of that cleanliness engulfed him.

Anirvan's inside was empty of tears. He had no more sadness left. Now he was poor.

'You little idiot,' the Lotus said. It was the sweetest voice in the world. 'Why are you crying?'

It was a voice that said that he loved Anirvan more for his tears. For his stupidity. He came close. He hugged Anirvan with his strong, fragrant arms; they snaked around the back of his neck and slid down to his back and drew him close. They slipped under his shirt and gently caressed him, rubbing his skin like they knew his flesh forever.

Miraculously, he strummed the sorrow out of his body.

'Your grandmother is an extraordinary woman.' His

voice deepened, its softness gone. 'She has gathered rare karma.'

'Really?' Anirvan's voice shivered.

'If you have trouble believing, just go and stand before the mirror.' There was ferocity in his voice, a sudden flash. 'Look at yourself. Who has made you? This beautiful boy?'

Anirvan closed his eyes. The Lotus sat him on his lap, slowly caressed his neck and shoulders. Roughly, he ran his fingers through his hair, squeezed clumps of it in his palm.

Anirvan felt his muscles through the thin saffron fabric; soft and strong muscles that were real, so real.

You have trained your grandson beautifully. His grandmother glowed like the sun every time she repeated what the Maharaj had told her, the very first time she came to the ashram. 'He saw it, right away. After all he is the Maharaj.' The saffron king who owned nothing.

'The day she leaves the earth, she will leave the cycle of karma altogether.' He looked away, past the balcony, to the silence left by the homing birds. 'Her soul will be free.'

She laughed and sang in the crowded hospital ward where everybody was going to die. It wasn't death. It was freedom.

'Come.' Kamal Swami gestured dismissively. 'Let's go.'

Anirvan walked next to him.

The Lotus led him into the prayer hall. He parted the thick curtain and stepped inside. The empty hall felt like a palace as Anirvan entered behind him. The air was dead and still inside, unlike how it usually was, full of music and incense and restless boys. The Swami went to the end of the hall, opened the wooden cupboard, and took out two prayer mats. He spread them out at the usual place, at the back of the hall near the wall.

'Sit.' He gestured towards the second mat. His voice was soft again, a voice that belonged to the prayer hall.

Anirvan sat down, folded his legs. He sat in the posture of lotus yoga. His spine was straight and limbs taut. He had returned to a natural state, and he looked not seated but afloat, on cool water.

'Think of your grandmother.' The Swami whispered. 'And let your mind cry.' His voice trailed off. He was leaving Anirvan.

'But only your mind.' He whispered again, almost inaudibly. 'Only inside. Only the tears of the mind.'

His chest rose and fell as he took deep breaths. 'Let your mind out. Let it get drunk with sorrow. Let it bathe in the mud of pain.' He took a deep breath. 'Step back. Watch the mind. The little toy.'

Anirvan lost his mind. The mind of the Yogi. It swam away from him. It became a liquid thing, a pool, and then a sea. A glowing blue sea.

When he opened his eyes, the prayer hall was full of boys. Restless, white cotton-draped boys who peeked back and stared at him. They started to whisper but stopped suddenly. The Lotus was still seated next to Yogi; a slow-breathing, blind statue.

Yogi's mind was back, fresh and clean and alive. He was calm and afloat.

There was beauty and power in saffron that no colour in this world could match.

Flesh

Bliss Hall was hit by a famine just as they entered Class
8. The immediate trigger was Tavi's lust for food. But
actually it was a long time coming.

Hunger was a pain. Everybody was always on the
prowl for meat. There was very little real food to go
around, round the clock.

Who could live forever with chunks of bread as thick
as brickbats with a brushing of butter on it? The dining
hall was a war zone and strange things happened at dinner
when after all the garbage of daal and vegetables, they
served a single egg. It was a beautiful, golden egg, boiled
to perfection and then fried in oil. Some people ate their
whole dinners just by staring at the egg which they placed
at a key corner of their plate, to be relished at the end, a
tiny bite at a time.

That night Tavi went overboard with the spitting and
claimed eggs that were not his own. Eggs were sensitive
things on the plate once they were served and suddenly
a boy's neighbour might just gasp at something terrible
outside the window. If the boy fell for it and looked away
from his plate there was no egg there anymore as his
laughing neighbour had already stuffed his mouth with

the golden egg. People did everything to save their eggs, hide it under the mounds of rice, sit with it in their left hand, even eat it the moment it touched the plate, which was hard as the rest of dinner was a long dry spell of pain after that. Tavi's style was brilliant. He spat all over his plate and drowned the egg in a fresh puddle of spit the moment it arrived on his plate and so it was safe from all invaders. Who wanted an egg coated with someone else's spit? The strategy worked too well and he got greedy. That night after spitting on his own egg he rolled up a mouthful of spittle and shot at the egg that had just landed on Lothar's plate right next to him, hoping to claim that one as well as nobody could possibly want to eat something wet with his spit.

Lothar was a sleeping volcano. Full of jingles and puns and a mudslinging pig on the football field. Who could tell there was such brutal anger inside? He took the egg and flung it at Tavi's face, and then he took the curried pumpkin and flung it at his face too, which was unkind as Tavi hated pumpkin.

Sushant Kane exploded and threw them both out of the dining room. It was confusing as he normally noticed nothing, chewed his food absently and left the dining hall without talking to anybody. He came early and left early; always before Kamal Swami entered. Sushant Kane looked strange these days, especially since Bora's beating, as if a red hot tip of rage was burning inside him.

'*Out!*' He stood before the table, a lanky messenger of death. 'Both of you.'

Tavi and Lothar stepped out, both smeared in curried

pumpkin, for Tavi had returned the love. The saddest thing was that two golden eggs lay on their plates, both drowned in Tavi's spit. Never to be eaten.

Even Pir was terrified when he saw them. Pir, the small boy from Mosulgaon who came in to help clean the kitchen and the dining hall for a meal. He was barely 8 or 9, but seemed to laugh at everything, steadfast in his claim that he could read palms to tell the future. The boys mocked him but still crowded to show him their palms. Everybody called him Pir. No one remembered his real name.

Even Pir was terrified.

Tavi and Lothar looked like orange demons at the door.

Sushant Kane left them standing outside the dining hall, their faces a gooey mess. And then he left. Kamal Swami would come soon. He would ask what the matter was. And then they would have to tell him.

Nobody knew what the Lotus did to them, but they returned to their rooms hungry. It was dangerous to have Tavi around in a state of hunger. Especially after lights-off when the teachers had locked themselves inside their rooms.

Along the terrace overlooking the block, pigeons had made wild nests. They slept inside the ventilators and soiled the ledge of the terrace with poop. One pigeon had dozed off in a low crevice on the wall of the block.

'We can get matches from Tridib sir's cupboard, right?' Tavi asked. Sharp light shone in his eyes.

The boys nodded.

'Let's gather all the waste paper in Lothar's room.'
Tavi whispered.

Catching the pigeon was easy. They were probably
night-blind. Quite stupid too. Could barely walk, let alone
fly. Tavi crept like a snake. Everybody held their breath.
Rajeev crept behind Tavi, though it was not clear why he
did that.

Tavi slunk a long arm into the crevice and pulled out
the pigeon. It was a large pigeon but it moved very little.
It was probably old, or sick. One wing fluttered clumsily
but Tavi clamped it hard. A few feathers fluttered to the
ground.

The matchbox and the heap of waste papers were
ready in Lothar's room. It was the middle room of the
block and far from the teacher's. And it belonged to
the messiest boy that had ever lived and his room was
cluttered with everything that could burn—torn pages of
books, old newspapers, lost socks, wrappers of chocolates
with brown gooey stuff on them.

A quiet crowd gathered. Rajeev gathered the heap of
paper in the heart of the room. The striking of the match
made a ghastly sound. The fire coiled up from the heap like
a snake that was slowly getting fat. The lazy pigeon burst
into a splatter of wings and feathers when Tavi brought
him closer to the fire.

'You can't put him there alive,' Rajeev whispered. 'You
need to bump him off.'

Tavi tried one more time. The pigeon beat hard in his
hand. In the silence, the noise shot out like an explosion.
Tavi clamped down hard. Beads of sweat on his forehead
shone in the fire.

He looked around.

Rajeev held out a heavy padlock to him. He could read Tavi's mind.

They stared in silence as Tavi bunched up the tail of the pigeon and smashed the padlock on his head and before they had a chance to see anything more he held the bird by the tail and hung it over the fire. The mashed head was safely inside.

It became much easier when Rajeev brought out the mustard oil that somebody kept handy for bathing. As the wings blackened, things started coming off in flakes. 'Just like chicken,' Bora said.

Asim Chatterjee pushed through the crowd. 'Salt and chilli.' He had popped his hand inside the kitchen window to grab a handful of salt. Chilli shrubs, they all knew, were plentiful behind the kitchen. When did he go down? He wasn't scared of waking up anybody. Kamal Swami, Nitai the caretaker, the teachers. That's because Chatterjee wasn't scared of anything. He had taught his roommates to rub their penises while looking at pictures of naked women from magazines.

Their hunger was shocking. There were no knives but someone got out a pair of scissors and started cutting out chunks of roasted meat. Chillies were split open and oil and salt splattered all over. 'Chicken night,' Bora whispered hoarsely and put the scissors with the piece of meat stuck to it in his mouth.

Anirvan was so disgusted that he couldn't stop staring. It was as if Lothar's room had become a butchery. The fire had died but Rajeev lit it again because the tail end of the pigeon was still raw and there was good meat there. Boys were now using their fingers to tear off the meat. Bones were chewed and spat out. They were smaller bones, lighter than those in chicken.

There were seven or eight boys in the room. More boys came in, rubbing sleep from their eyes. Chatterjee wanted to catch more pigeons. 'Sami has hot and sour Maggi ketchup in his room.' Sami was the son of the Chief Justice and he couldn't eat his lunch without ketchup so he was allowed to take ketchup to the dining hall. 'Let's catch a baby pigeon. Tender meat.' Chatterjee smacked his lips. 'Will be yummy with ketchup.'

But that didn't happen. Tridib was three rooms away and even though he slept like dead wood it was risky climbing over the balcony and walking on the ledge to poke through the nests. But there was nothing left of the pigeon that they had cooked. Even the bones were a chewed mess.

Anirvan thought of Kajol's sleeping face. He'd stopped by his room on his way to Lothar's. The room was dark but faint light from the corridor fell through the mosquito net. Kajol slept like he had left the world for a better place. His long eyelashes were still. He fell asleep the moment the bell rang for lights-off and slept unstirred till the first tingle of the morning bell. Never ruffled by a nightmare. Or the need to leave his bed in the middle of the night to go to another boy's room.

Kajol wasn't here. Kajol would never do something like this.

Bora offered Anirvan a slice of meat. 'Better than chicken,' he said. 'Eat na.'

Anirvan liked Bora. He was a wild animal, but if you got him to talk he became a different person. He talked about his father whom he called Dragon as when he lost his temper he didn't stop till he had flayed some of his son's skin with his metal-studded leather belt. Of his little sister whom he loved very much.

Anirvan ate the meat. It was soft and slippery. Very soft. Pungent with smoke and mustard oil and full of chilli seeds. He liked it.

He thought of the prayer hall, a room made of pure white cotton and saffron and the curling smoke of incense.

Anirvan went to Sushant Kane's room the next afternoon. He had to return a book. *Tess of the D'Urbervilles*. He loved the book even though he didn't really understand it. He could speak in its language if he tried.

A liquid bond with language. That's what SrK called it. Anirvan felt special. Sushant Kane lit up something inside him even though everything about it was wrong—his anger and cigarettes and the bitter words that twisted his mouth. But he lit up before Anirvan—he loved Anirvan's slippery friendship with words. Anirvan longed to make him proud. One day he would. One day, he would speak to the world. He would.

'The boys ate a pigeon last night,' he told him. He wanted to tell him everything. All the time. Because no matter what you told him, SrK had something strange to say in response.

'What?' He frowned. He looked ill when he did that.

'Tavi caught a pigeon from the ledge.' Anirvan said nervously. 'They roasted it in Lothar's room.'

SrK threw the book down. Disgust seeped off his face like cigarette smoke.

'What the bloody...!' He couldn't finish the sentence.

'Everybody was hungry,' Anirvan said quickly. 'Of course, Tavi and Lothar didn't even eat their eggs.'

'Bloody crazy,' SrK finished his sentence.

'Keep growing boys on meagre food. And then push them to play football all the way to nirvana!' He said, frowning at the wall. 'They know very well the body has needs. They know it all.'

Maniacally, he whispered, like he wanted to talk to Anirvan but couldn't.

'The brotherhood of monks!' He hissed. 'The brotherhood of bodily needs!'

He looked at his watch. Then he took off his home kurta, put on a shirt, and picked up his wallet and cigarettes.

Fear rose like a cloud around Anirvan, eating and gulping everything. But he couldn't leave SrK. Like an iron filling, he was stuck to the madman. He wanted to see it all.

'Come with me,' SrK said.

They left the hostel and walked past the lawns, and then past all the hostels toward the main ashram stadium, where the big inter-college and state level cricket and football matches happened. Anirvan wondered why they were going to the stadium but he could not ask him. But

Sushant Kane turned right just before the stadium and they walked into this narrow lane that wove past the walls. Anirvan had no idea where this lane went as the boys were not allowed to come here.

He felt excited. And a little anxious. Where were they going? Would he be back in the hostel before Kajol came back? They showered together every evening, meditating under the rain.

The lane opened onto the main road. Anirvan's heart beat wildly. Stepping out was against the rule. If a boy was caught, he could be expelled. Didn't Sushant Kane know that? Was it okay if you went out with a teacher? There were no guards on this side. This gate was more of a crack in the wall. Would someone tell the monks if they saw them?

Sushant Kane hailed an autorickshaw.

'Tejpur,' he told the driver. He nodded and they hopped in.

He groped inside his pocket and took out his packet of Gold Flake cigarettes and a box of matches. Anirvan had never actually seen him smoke, only smelled cigarettes on him. He had imagined him smoking many times, especially inside the cool darkness of his room. Did he really smoke in there? Anirvan couldn't imagine what might happen if one of the monks saw him smoking.

He opened the packet and Anirvan was shocked. There was a dirty bunch of bidis inside. Why would he smoke these horribly rustic rolled up dry leaves stuffed with tobacco? Only coolies and servants smoked bidis. And what kind of a person hid bidis inside a shiny packet of Gold Flake cigarettes?

He lit the bidi and puffed at it. Bright red fire sparked at the tip and there was a horrible dusty odour. He held the bidi like a railway station coolie might. The auto chugged over potholes—this was a remote suburb and the roads were barely hewn out of the earth. Clouds of dust flew at their face as they rolled along the unmade path.

They stopped next to a shop. It was a roadside stall with a thatched roof.

It was a sleepy kind of an eatery. There were odd-shaped tables inside the smoky darkness of the interior. Spiky straw stuck out at places on the wall and dark men in undershirts moved around silently.

Half the eatery jutted out on the road, where a group of men sat silently with a pack of cards and small glasses of milky tea. SrK and Anirvan went inside and sat at one of the tables.

'Two plates of meat curry and paratha,' SrK called out.

Anirvan was hit by delight. Meat curry and paratha from a street stall was an absurd dream at the ashram.

And then his delight vanished. He remembered.

'I didn't really eat the pigeon,' He whispered. 'I wasn't hungry.'

'I just had a tiny piece.' Anirvan couldn't lie to him. 'Bora kept asking.'

'Do they really believe they are producing mini-monks? Young men who can live on roots and water and don't need hot water or electric fans?' He stared at Anirvan, but he wasn't talking to him. 'They are producing animals.'

'Save the world from designer poverty!' He looked up and it seemed like he was praying, a praying man crying to the sky. 'Someday you're going to see those who have nothing to eat. That day you'll have something real to say.'

Anirvan didn't know what to say. His ears felt warm.

'The world is not just incense and flowers and the loving touch,' SrK said. 'Loving and caressing and fondling.' The words flew like spit from his mouth.

A small boy came with two plates of paratha and two bowls of curry. Pir? Suddenly, Anirvan felt a punch in his brain. Pir, here?

Pir placed the food on their table and stood there, grinning. He was in his usual khaki shorts and white t-shirt, an old PT uniform the Mission boys had discarded. He didn't look surprised at all. Would he tell? The next time he was in the Bliss Hall dining room?

'Eat.' Sushant Kane gestured toward the plate.

Yogi sat there, frozen.

Pir stood there, smiling.

'Pir!' Sushant Kane laughed. 'Don't you worry, he's smarter than you. Sees much and says little.'

Anirvan had not washed his hands. How could he eat?

SrK tore into a paratha. 'Go ahead, eat,' he said.

Anirvan rubbed his hands against his pants. Rubbed them hard. He hadn't really touched anything that dirty. He tore a piece of paratha and dipped it into the gravy. He could not bear to savour the meat. Yet. It was too precious.

Sushant Kane wrapped a piece of meat in paratha, drowned it in gravy, and put it in his mouth.

He did the same. As he bit into the meat he knew

it was different. He knew the kind. And that it was not goat.

He stopped chewing. He stared at Sushant Kane. He frowned. 'What happened?'

'It's beef,' he said and resumed chewing. 'You eat beef, don't you?'

It was easier to say 'beef'. You didn't have to say 'cow meat'.

He nodded. He had eaten beef before. Tutul Gupta brought pasta and meatballs from home sometimes and Yogi always took a few bites when he was his roommate. Yogi's father had also taken him to Rahmania in Park Street once to have spicy beef curry. That's how he knew the taste. The flabbier, leathery feel of the meat as opposed to softer, flakier chunks of goat meat.

But always beef. Never cow meat.

Beef disgusted his mother. And his grandmother…he couldn't imagine a world where she knew that he and his father had eaten cow meat. He imagined her still eyes, heavy with tears.

He would never be able to tell this to Kamal Swami. He would die of shame if the Swami came to know.

'Sure you have.' Sushant Kane snorted. 'Guys who smash a pigeon's head with a padlock and roast it will eat anything!'

A tiny shiver ran through Anirvan's spine. How did he know about the padlock? Anirvan hadn't told him.

True, they were savages. They had tried to burn that pigeon alive. It didn't want to burn. This was a breath of the normal. A dusty roadside restaurant, deep-fried paratha and spicy beef curry. The cheap meat. For the poor people who lived in Mosulgaon and other villages in the area.

He ate. He was hungry. Not just that moment and hour, but for days and months. When you live with hunger for months and months and fill your stomach with a sea of daal and a forest of spinach, you get hungry for the oily stench of meat in a way that shocks and pleases you.

'Kane!' A voice called out from the darkness of the hotel.

The man came closer. He was tall and large. He might have once been an athlete. Now muscle and flab blended to hang loosely on him but he still moved with a sinewy smoothness. He came and sat down next to them. 'The boy from the ashram?'

'Yes.' Sushant Kane said. 'A rather interesting boy from the ashram.'

'How'd you whisk him away? Do the sadhus know?'

Sushant Kane's face cracked with disgust. As if the food suddenly nauseated him. 'They had a riot on their hands.'

'Riot?' The man frowned. 'At the ashram?'

'Boys versus pigeons,' Sushant Kane talked and chewed. 'Boys setting pigeons on fire.'

The man laughed, sending swirls of booming music up in the air. 'The little monks! Early start in the cult of animal slaughter!'

Anirvan could eat no more. He was chewing a cow and he knew it. The hump on the animal's back loomed large in front of him. The hump rich with meat now in his mouth.

'Big burly boys.' Sushant Kane wiped his plate clean with the last scrap of paratha. 'They just want to drown them in a sea of piss-like daal.'

'Oh, I don't know about that.' Suddenly, the man's face darkened. 'Plenty of boys from these villages are in the ashram on scholarships. They like the daal there.'

'You must be from the city.' He narrowed his eyes at Anirvan. 'Aren't you?'

Anirvan nodded.

'I know the food they give you at the ashram,' the man said. 'It's good stuff. I know many boys who study there. But they are all from the villages.'

Anirvan didn't know what to say.

'But you guys miss all the fancy noodles and chilli chicken and biryani and chocolates that you get at home every day. Don't you? No matter how much your parents stuff you every Sunday?'

Everything grew warm inside Anirvan. This was true and it wasn't.

'There are boys who would kill to get the food you throw away.' The man stared at him with dead eyes. 'Good sport, isn't it, to see who can throw away the most rice down the drain?'

How did he know? They had been blue with rage after the shutdown of the cricket match on TV and had longed to devastate the ashram, loot and plunder. Pretending to eat, they had thrown plates and plates of rice down the gutters behind the sink outside the dining hall. Rice and daal and all the vegetables they had served, carefully, pretending to walk out when the teachers were not looking. Pir had stared at them in wonder. They had thrown away more rice than he had ever seen in his village. The gutter had been white with rice, like a brown shrine covered with flowers.

Anirvan thought of Pir's face. The boy who saw more than he said.

The half-eaten meat curry grew cold before Anirvan. He glanced at Sushant Kane. He was looking at Anirvan. As if he had a question he didn't know how to ask.

Anirvan stared at the man.

'But you've never lived in the ashram,' he said. 'What do you know?'

'I know more than you'll ever do,' the man smiled.

'We get up at 5.30 in the morning every day,' Anirvan said. 'We run around the fields and do arches and sit-ups and push-ups for forty-five minutes. We come back to our rooms and change into the white dhotis and chadors and go into the prayer hall and sing and pray for another half an hour and then head to the study hall where we crack algebra and chemistry for an hour and a half. And then we have school all day after which we play football to get closer to god. And then we study all evening because the monthlies are always around the corner and then the half-yearly and the annual where we score so high that our math teachers burst with pride.'

'Yeah, yeah, I know that,' the man looked at him with sleepy eyes. 'Papa and mamma leaning over the little geniuses with pasta and meatballs from five-star hotels and chocolates sent over by uncles and aunts in Europe. Such hardship.'

He looked at Sushant Kane who was puffing urgently at a smelly bidi. 'I know these boys. From these villages, some from the Sunderban forests, poor tribal boys. They just go around beating a football in the sun while their classmates, these princes get mommies to stuff them with keema paratha while their daddies solve their geometry problems. Fucking hard life.'

Sushant Kane said nothing. He just puffed at the bidi and flicked smoke on the yellow stains on his empty plate, the drying gravy of the dead cow they had just eaten.

But it went away. Melted and gone. The dark, smoky interior of that eatery, the bamboo poles that held up the thatched roof, wooden benches that looked like shed snakeskin. Anirvan was back in the prayer hall where there was no yellow beef-stain but the mild laughter of the Happy Bearded One and the mild memory of oysters which The Bearded One ate as it was good for the heart. Or was it the lungs? It was him, Anirvan. *Yogi.* He sat on the dark, ribbed carpet and floated in the white, meandering hair of incense smoke and there was song around him, even though the prayer hall was totally empty. But his body didn't touch the carpet, just a cushion of air above it and when he touched his knees he felt the smoothness of the saffron robes and the memory of Kajol's long eyebrows like a sliver of pain.

'You won't understand the place,' Yogi looked into the man's eyes and paused, and spoke softly. 'There are the eyes of the bird who sits on her eggs to warm them. Her eyes look blank, says the prophet. She cares nothing for the world; all of her is in her eggs, to warm her babies to life. Such are the eyes of the Yogi. Dead and blank. All for god and none for the world. Hundreds of pairs of such eyes you see in our ashram. Going about, living the everyday and finishing homework and cracking puzzles in math and physics. Eyes dead and gone.'

Coarse and dirty smoke from Sushant Kane's bidi flooded Yogi's nostrils and he wanted to vomit. SrK was listening to everything, hanging on to every word. He was, wasn't he? He really was.

There was a shine in the man's eyes like the tip of a dog's nose when he licks it.

'They're smoking something bad at the ashram, real bad,' the man looked at Anirvan, unblinking. 'Or is he some kind of freak?'

'He's a great kid. A super kid we need to pull out of the toxic fumes of their incense sticks before they get to him. The drugged brotherhood.' Sushant Kane stubbed out his bidi on his yellow-stained plate and looked at Yogi. 'Finish your meat and then we've got to head back. Evening prayer starts in twenty minutes.'

'I don't want to eat any more.' Yogi stared at the chunks of meat in the dull steel bowl. The gravy had thickened to a flesh of its own.

He was seized by a quiet fury. He wanted to drill holes in this man. Who was he? He was an adversary. He would strangle Anirvan with a cloud of words. But Yogi would strangle him back.

As they walked toward the auto-rickshaw, Sushant Kane blew more sickening smoke in his face.

'You were in the mood for an adda!' He said. 'Not a speech, just a chatty chat.'

Anirvan's head reeled in the smoke and words refused to come. Dreamily, he wanted to reach out to that man, weave a web of words that would throttle him to a blue death. He wanted to talk to him again.

The Fragrance of Paan

The little book of Gita rose and fell on his grandmother's chest. It was no longer a human body. It made an animal noise.

She was no more in the world. There was a bit of breath trapped in her that made her room an echo chamber of howls. But she was already past pain. She wasn't anybody he knew.

It was late afternoon and nobody was home. His grandmother's last nurse was a Vaishnavi woman who smeared her nose and forehead with sandalwood paste and ash and other ghostly things. She never spoke much to others but always hummed and sang to herself.

She had placed a dusty booklet of the Gita on his grandmother's chest. They did such things. Throw flowers and incense sticks on corpses, dress them up with garlands. Place cheap copies of the Gita. Was this a corpse? A corpse that still breathed?

The mad Vaishnavi nurse had done what needed to be done. There was nobody else.

He stood next to the gasping corpse. Looked at her for a long time. He could not look away from the Gita dancing on her chest.

Then he left.

He was home for the Saraswati Puja weekend. The festival of Saraswati, the goddess of learning. The narrow lanes were fragrant and musical. Girls roamed in red-bordered saris and there were heaps of flowers outside the pandals. Whatever remained from the morning prayers.

As he roamed, he heard the shivering voice of his grandmother singing the hymn for goddess Saraswati. *Her breasts adorned with pearls.* The veena in one hand, a book in the other. *Pearls adorning her breasts.*

He roamed and roamed. Following the wilderness of scented flowers in the neighbourhood streets, walking along the slivers of music trailing off the loudspeakers. He waited.

People were back in the house when he returned. She had died.

The corpse was still.

They were busy. She had to be burned quickly.

Anirvan didn't have to go through any of the smelly mess they did to the body after it died. Or he didn't remember it if he did. He was returned to the ashram. It didn't seem to make much sense for him to prolong his stay in that house now that she was dead.

He was in the prayer hall, alone. He didn't know what he was doing there. He felt the empty hall touch and soothe him. There were all these portraits on the wall, all around the hall. Strange men with dazed looks and

chadors around their chests. They were disciples of the
Happy Bearded One. Some of them looked bewildered; a
few looked grim; others looked at peace. Garlands hugged
these photos but they looked dried and yellowed. They
were changed far less often than those at the main shrine
in front where the trinity sat: the Happy Bearded One
at the centre, the Great Saffron One to his right and the
Melting Mother to his left.

The floor of the prayer hall was a huge white bed.
Thick, ribbed carpets covered in thick white chador, the
same kind that covered the boys' bodies. The shrine was
white too. White chador, white flowers, the white of the
Melting Mother's sari and the thin red border. The creased
robe of the Great Saffron One was a dull flame.

The windows of the prayer hall were small; most of
them covered with thin curtains that flapped in the wind.
The outside was not allowed in. The prayer hall was its
own sky. The weight of his body vanished. He was afloat
in air even though the fans were turned off; they swayed
softly in the air streaming through the windows. It was the
kind of wide and sunny room that made one breathless.

Tears rolled down his cheeks. He was alone and he
could tell the prayer hall anything. These walls held the
scent of god.

He went to the back, opened the cupboard and took
out the prayer mat that looked like a tiger skin. He spread
it out next to the wall and sat down on it, right next to the
Lotus, who sat there, his spine stretched, arms stretched
over his knees, eyes closed. He didn't see Anirvan.

Anirvan closed his eyes and breathed deeply. In. Out.

In. Out. In. Out. They rose and fell like seawaves. His body was no longer human.

But something held him back. The flapping, butterfly-yellow of the curtains at the small windows. The whiteness of the chadors fragrant with incense. Something in him didn't want to leave this room.

But he was alone. He had to rise above the earth.

'When an ant dies,' Kamal Swami spoke, his eyes still closed. 'It returns to the earth as a fly in its next birth.'

'When the fly dies, it is reborn as a grasshopper.'

'It may become a human being after a hundred births.'

'Humans are mired beings. They float from one life to another. They cannot give up the pleasures of the body. Great Brahmins who have spent their lives in prayer come back to earth for the taste of sweet yogurt. You know the babies who have a sweet tooth from their birth, don't you?'

He didn't wait for Anirvan to speak. He went on.

'Gold threads on red saris. The feel of blankets made of goose feathers. The memory of bright chandeliers. Everything brings the spirit back. To be reborn.'

His eyes were still closed. Trancelike, he spoke.

'The day your grandmother walked into my room, I knew there was nothing that could hold her spirit to earth.'

But Yogi thought of paan. Fragrant green leaves stuffed with mildly intoxicating spices that reddened the shriveled lips of the old woman, jaws that moved constantly. And sweets—she could not go to bed without a piece of cream-carved love from one of the neighbourhood shops. Would she come back for them?

Be a little kindhearted newborn with paan-stained teeth and a craving for fried sweets?

'She's not to come back,' Kamal Swami's slow, whispering words made his heart jump. 'She's not to come back.'

'She was not of this world. She belonged to the Godhead.'

'She loved you,' the monk turned and touched his shoulder. 'You were made by her love. But she was made of something...something that is not forged in this world. She lived outside the cycle of karma. Even while she lived here.'

Warmth flooded the innards of his body. She was his grandmother. He was made by her love.

She was ethereal. Far beyond the grimy garland of karma.

'Seven generations before him,' a smiling old woman voice flooded his head. 'And seven generations after attaining nirvana. Fourteen generations in all, freed from the cycle of death and rebirth.'

'If a boy puts on the robes of a monk.'

Who said that? He opened his eyes, looked at the Lotus. He couldn't be sure. Was it the voice in his head? Was it the Lotus? The soft cotton fabric was his skin. Happy. Kind. Calm.

'The brotherhood of love.' The Swami said softly. 'Kajol knows that. Doesn't he?'

Yes, he did. Yes, they did.

He wanted to lie down on the bed of saffron.

Widowhood

Kajol's hug was home. He hugged Yogi hard. It grew harder, as if Kajol was trying to flush out the pain in his chest. He dreaded looking at Yogi's face, at the cheeks on which tears had dried. He would lick his cheeks wet again, wet with the shine of pain. He would make Yogi his own.

Kajol was real. He would always be real. He would be there, like a quiet whisper in Yogi's ears. *Always.* Yogi closed his eyes and nuzzled the side of Kajol's bony neck. Soap and clean cotton and the heartwarming Kajol smell.

'I don't want to go play today,' Kajol said. His eyes grew wet.

'Really, don't worry,' Yogi said. 'Go. I'll be fine.'

'No,' Kajol said. 'No way.'

'Why ask for trouble? They're going to notice you're not on the field and then Mihir Dam will mark you absent and you'll be in a spot.'

Yogi fought for words. It was so hard to fight Kajol. This Kajol who suddenly looked mired in tears and a red film of anger. Anger at not being able to claw his way out of it. Yogi had never heard him speak of school rules as if he cared so little about them. But it was impossible to see Kajol break rules and suffer from the wreck.

'Kajol,' he begged. 'I'll be fine, just go play.'

He didn't want Kajol around. He felt naked in his pain, a spiky mess. He wanted to curl up and die.

But he had no idea Kajol could do such things. Did he not care about school rules after all? What was he willing to throw away? This was not a boy Yogi knew.

'You can't make me go.' Kajol stared at him.

He had moved closer to Yogi. Closer still. On him was the musky sweat of the afternoon, end-of-the-school-day sweat. Longing for the violent sweat of the playground.

Kajol wanted to melt into Yogi. But Yogi wanted distance today. Distance from touching, from breath and sweat.

Yogi clasped his wrist. The thin breakable bone.

'Really, Kajol,' he looked straight into his eyes. 'Let me be. I have to clear my head. I just need to wander and think of her for a while.'

Kajol looked at him unhappily. His eyes softened.

He left. He didn't look back.

Yogi took a long time to tie the laces of his running shoes. It was hard to be at it for so long. He had to tie it up all wrong, get it knotted up, and then undo the tangle. While doing the left shoe he forgot and tied the laces up properly. Quickly, he looked up to see if anyone was around. And then he untied it and knotted it all in a tangle. And so it took a long time.

When he was done, everybody was gone. Their block

was empty. As he walked down the stairs, as slowly as he could, he realized, there were no boys left in Bliss Hall; everybody had reached the football fields by now. He would have been there too, only if he hadn't made such a mess with his shoelaces.

Between four and six every day, the boys from all classes had to gather in the sports fields. If any boy was found anywhere in the hostel, he would be punished. It was a rule everybody had forgotten was a rule. They couldn't wait to be at the football fields and bash around the mud with the ball.

He had lost the will and the muscle to keep up the game. Nothing mattered after death.

They were in such a hurry that they never noticed he was taking forever to tie his laces. When on the sports field, the boys noticed nothing.

Nobody knew a boy could try to flee football. Nitai the caretaker saw him straggling along the stairs of the empty hostel, and said, 'Poor thing, still here? Just dash to the field! They've barely just started.'

He had to be careful on the road. It wound past the other hostels and then turned right toward the school. You had to keep to that road and the playgrounds would come up right opposite the school. But instead of turning right, he turned left. He went over the little bridge that ran over the half-dried canal below. Then he entered the large building to the left.

It was the Central Library. The main library of the ashram. It was a huge house. He always slipped in there like an elf. People came there from the college and from outside the ashram and in a way it felt like a part of the big real world outside its walls and nobody bothered to check who you were and where you were from. Sometimes he worried that people would stare at him not just because he looked too small but he was there in his sports outfit and white running shoes but no one cared. They just checked your bags thoroughly before you left so there was no chance of stealing a book. He was in love with those little, clothbound, gold-embossed editions of old English novels they had and used to look longingly at the windows inside and dream. If only the slats were wide enough, he would toss one out in order to pick it up later when he was outside. *The Mayor of Casterbridge*. Little, smooth and blue, with gold lettering and a gold thread as a bookmark. There was much in the Central Library to steal and some people stole them. That was the only place in the ashram you could read the adult novels published in the special festival issues of magazines; but sometimes just as you came to the naughty parts you found the pages torn. It was a large library and the reading rooms were often nearly empty and it was not hard to tear pages out and stuff them in your pockets because they would never catch them while checking your bags. When he came to those torn pages, he wanted to chop their hands off.

As he walked into the library he knew where to go. Rows of ochre-coloured volumes sat on the shelves next to the windows. Large volumes with white flowers painted on the top. He knew them from home. They lay scattered in his grandmother's room. His widowed aunt who lived in Asansol had the entire series. She brought a

volume whenever she visited and took back the one his
grandmother had finished reading.

They were the stories of the old Bengali writer
Saratchandra, mostly about pain and suffering and sorrow,
especially of women in villages with wicked landlords and
cruel Brahmins, full of good people who suffered. The
suffering was magnetic and engrossing.

They drew him in. Saratchandra's language was old-
fashioned but easy and felt wet and shiny with tears
and he slipped deep inside his stories; the slow, saintly
verbs became his own. He couldn't actually speak in that
language as it would be too strange to break out in a
language found in books possibly written a hundred years
ago but he could, he easily could if he wanted. Even Kamal
Swami would be confused if he spoke in that language but
he would love Yogi more if he found out that Yogi could
speak in a tongue a little closer to Sanskrit.

Today he could only reach out to these stories. He
wanted to be with the kind, white-clad widows, even
the wicked ones that chewed paan and laughed with
blackened teeth. They surely craved for cream-carved
sweets even though back in those days widows were not
allowed to crave anything.

He pulled out a book and sat down. He opened to a
story called 'The Brahmin's Daughter'. It was a story of
such dark and sad pain that it cinched him like a drug. It
was about how a rich old Brahmin man tortured a young
female relative of his, a helpless widow. Nobody could
change anything and in the end she suffered a terrible
tragedy. It was dark because Yogi didn't quite understand

what he did to her, something which made her want to kill herself. The most evil figure in the story was that of a woman, an old widow in white who knew a rich Brahmin could do no wrong no matter what he did. She coaxed and cajoled the young widow to let the rich Brahmin do what he wanted with her. While reading, he always imagined the old widow with a big round head, closely shaven, covered with the coarse white cotton of the widow's sari. She was nothing like his grandmother. His grandmother wore white saris of fine quality that had a thin coloured border around them. But still it was the widow that drew him to that story today. The pain she caused to the young woman, a pain that was hard to understand and impossible to bear.

Saratchandra's stories were like wet moss. There were village ponds and muddy rivers and thatched huts and the dark empty rooms in the houses of rich landlords. Fruits ripened and spread their drowsy smell, women gossiped by the pond and untouchables swept their own footsteps away so that Brahmins didn't have to step on them. It was a sad world now dead and gone.

There was one of these books lying on the desk in his grandmother's room that no one had dusted for years. Dust was a thick layer on the plastic table cloth that no one had changed forever. She had not read the book for several weeks now. She had been too sick.

The widows in the stories were like ghosts. They were silent women with shaved heads; garrulous and crooked; fat and old; young and beautiful—their beauty impossible and sinister because they were widows.

He was haunted by the teenage widow who felt her

lips burn when they were kissed by a man, because she had fallen in love with him. Her name was Lolita, wasn't it? What was the name of that story? His heart jumped when her lips burned, and now all widows had a touch of Lolita in them, lurking behind like a half-eaten beam of moonlight.

'What are you reading?'

The hand on his shoulder startled him.

It took him a while to recognize the voice while he stared at the fingers lingering over his right shoulder; bony fingers that curled like a spider, mild hair above the knuckles and a ring with a large green stone.

'The Brahmin's Daughter,' Sushant Kane stooped and looked at the book, turned the volume around. 'Saratchandra again?' A faint frown creased his forehead.

He knew everything Yogi liked to read and yet Yogi always felt a little shy showing him what he was reading. SrK liked to frown a lot. But there was no bitterness in the frown. It was acrid in a pleasant way, like the odour of tobacco that hung around him.

SrK liked to talk about books with Yogi. He used words Yogi did not understand, and yet Yogi always understood him. Yogi told him things that he liked in books, and SrK stared at him, his frown gone. He would say nothing about him sitting in the Central Library in his sports clothes and white running shoes, though Yogi knew he noticed all that. Yogi was cheating and breaking the rules of the Mission and SrK was happy whenever a boy cheated. But he didn't want SrK to catch him reading today as he didn't know what to do with his love for

Saratchandra's widows. It was a soppy, tearful kind of a love and he wanted to wipe his tears before SrK saw him, even though there were no real tears.

'I'm going to check out a few books,' SrK said. 'Then you can come with me.'

Yogi couldn't take his eyes off the large green stone on SrK's knuckle. His fingers opened and closed slowly, like the scrawny legs of a spider. A speck of a green forest at the heart of the spider.

He went up to the circulation desk. Yogi flushed the wet widow off his soul and closed the book. The white, entwining flowers on the ochre cover stared at him and there was a dull pain in his chest. There was no dust on the cover. They took good care of it.

Sushant Kane was back with a couple of books under his arms, bound library volumes. Yogi stood up and went with him.

SrK knew he was hiding in the library. Hiding in the library till game hour was over and he could return to Bliss Hall. The boys had to be on the field during this time. They could not wander around the campus. Nobody thought of looking into the Central Library. It was not even part of the school.

But it was okay if you were with a teacher. Sometimes Sushant Kane walked him out of the Central Library. They walked around the campus. SrK knew Yogi couldn't leave the library unless he took him out.

They walked out of the library. They walked over the little bridge that arched over the dead canal like a famous painting.

'I'm surprised that you like Saratchandra so much,' Sushant Kane said. 'Depressing stuff, isn't it?'

'I like reading the stories,' Yogi said. 'Like sliding along a tree-trunk moist with rain.'

It felt powerful when he spoke with words touched by Sanskrit. Like he was seated high above a snow-capped mountain.

'Are you all right?' Sushant Kane looked at him, alarmed. 'What are you, Kalidas?'

Mischief gurgled through Yogi. There was something funny about being with SrK, something warmly funny. SrK thought he was reciting an ancient Sanskrit poet. 'It's Saratchandra. Srikanta I think.' Possibly. Lots of tree trunks, lots of rain and dark flooding rivers in those stories.

'You soak up the virus pretty quick!' He looked away with sudden indifference. 'Last week you sounded like Thomas Hardy.'

Last week Yogi had longed to smuggle one of Hardy's beautiful gold-embossed tiny novels through the library window. But he didn't tell SrK any of that.

'This week it's different.'

'It's fine as a circus trick.' Sushant Kane said. 'But you are not a circus animal. When you have something real to say, you won't sound like a well-trained parrot.'

'What do you mean?' Yogi asked, confused.

'You're the best debater the school has ever seen,' he said. 'You don't know how deadly your talent is.'

There was something he wanted Yogi to do with his skill. As if he didn't really notice the debate competitions.

As if they were children's sport, just a wait for something else. Something bigger was in wait. It excited and terrified Yogi. What was he staring at?

Yogi wanted to say something but suddenly they came across Ari Swami and his boys. Three of them were always with him. Tutul Gupta, whose father owned a publishing house that brought out popular comics based on mythological stories. Tirtho Mukherjee, whose mother owned nothing but was a beautiful and talkative woman abandoned by her husband a long time ago. Plato Sen, who was a bit notorious, not only because he was terrible in studies, but also because his father had died mysteriously a couple of years ago in the middle of a corporate squabble.

They were all good-looking boys. Tutul and Tirtho were very fair, Plato was darker, but they all had the quality the monks liked—soft and perfectly hairless in Class 7. Their skin felt smooth if you caressed them.

Ari Swami was the perfect monk for this group. He was the headmaster of the school, a fair and handsome monk who must be much older than their fathers. He laughed in a booming way and said sharp and intelligent things in a beautiful rustic accent.

Sushant Kane slowed down as he saw Ari Swami.

'Hello, Sushant!' Ari Swami waved his affectionate smile in their direction.

Sushant Kane slowed down and smiled, raised his right hand in half a salute. He did not speak.

They walked past the group. Tutul, Tirtho and Plato didn't seem to notice Yogi. They noticed nothing. They didn't need to. They were Ari Swami's special boys.

Sometimes he wondered what it took to be one of Ari Swami's special boys. They were not good students. In fact, Tirtho was a poor student who had dirty habits. Plato was really dumb. Tutul was okay but nothing striking. There was only the slippery smoothness of their skin. Yogi could not think of anything else.

'Ari Swami is very fond of these boys,' he said.

Sushant Kane walked in silence.

'Of course,' he spat out the words. 'They melt when he touches them.'

His mood was bruised. The air felt raw.

In silence, they entered Bliss Hall. Yogi wondered whether to follow him to his room. It was best not to, not today.

Dancer, Lover, Sufferer

Kamal Swami chose Yogi to be the new prayer hall leader just as they entered Class 9.

He had chosen him. He was telling him something. Why would he make him the leader? The Lotus was the kind of hostel warden who plotted every assignment on the duty roster each month. He didn't consult the teachers living in Bliss Hall. Sushant Kane didn't care about any of that.

The Lotus was calling him. Yogi just had to close his eyes and he could see him, looking at him through his light, steel-framed glasses, smiling, clean-shaven with a green hue on his cheeks, with a shaved head but looking like he had a wild mane of black hair. There was a crowd of boys, and yet he was looking at Yogi.

He *had* to speak to the Swami. He had waited too long.

The prayer hall leader led a team of five boys who had to prepare the hall for the daily prayers. They would roll out the carpets for the boys to sit and pray; light the incense sticks; throw away yesterday's flowers and arrange fresh flowers on the shrine. On special days the prayer hall boys had to go out into the ashram gardens and pick flowers. The blood-red Joba flowers for the worship of

goddess Kali, orange marigold for goddess Durga, white
Champaka flowers for Shiva and the Great Saffron One,
who was like Shiva in many ways.

A big day was coming up. Janmashtami, the birthday
of Krishna. What was Krishna's favourite flower? They
grew somewhere in the ashram, surely. Everything grew
in the ashram. Every nook and cranny had a garden or
an orchard. And no one could ever make out where the
ashram began or ended, for it was everywhere. It was built
on the land of eighty-two villages. There were neighbours
who hated the ashram, calling it the land-thief. Such as
the villagers of Mosulgaon. The boys had all seen the
graffiti on the wall outside the stadium, splashed like
blood-streak. *Land-thieving monks. Give our homes back.*

'You two,' Kamal Swami's eyes had sparkled. 'Go and
look for the flowers on Friday.'

Thrill had shot through Yogi like a drug. He had stolen
a glance at Kajol. Kajol's eyes shone but he was quiet.

They would comb through the campus. Walking for
an hour or more, past the school for disabled children,
past the college, even beyond the crafts centre set up for
the welfare of the villages, past the Poultry and the Dairy
and the Teachers' Quarters and the huge stadium and
the narrow lovers' lane that wound around it. Whatever
it took.

'We'll go in the morning,' Kajol had said.

'Get up early and go,' the Swami said. 'Make the day
yours. Make Krishna happy.'

Kajol's eyes glistened. Looking at him, Yogi already
felt the smell of the rare flower, suddenly close at hand.

Kajol loved roaming the ashram with him. It was their own place, in a way no other place in the world would ever be theirs.

'I know my way around all the gardens.' Kajol said.

Was there a tinge of sadness in his voice? Where else could they be together but in the wilderness of the ashram?

'We'll find the flower,' Kajol said.

His voice floated.

But would it make Krishna happy? Making Krishna happy was never easy. The more you loved him the more he made you suffer.

Janmashtami was only a few days away. It was going to be a special, long prayer that would eat up some of their study hour. There would be many songs, all about Krishna. Yogi's heart beat faster at the thought. These songs held him in a spell. Krishna was blue and cruel and mesmeric.

Today he rushed to the prayer hall. He was the leader and he had to be the first one there. He also loved being in the prayer hall when it was empty.

But when he walked into the prayer hall, Mataal was dancing inside. There was no music but Mataal never needed music to dance. Music played in his head all the time.

Mataal was in the prayer hall team. His real name was Bijit—a boy with curly hair who lisped like a baby and liked to dance. Sometimes he danced in his room, curling his wrist and fingers in the mudras of classical dance.

When he danced, he looked drunk and dopey, and so he was called Mataal—the drunkard.

Why was he there so early? Yogi was supposed to be there before anyone else and wake the prayer hall up slowly, open the windows and clear up the closed air from the night. Start to sweep and mop the floor. That's when his boys would walk in. Yogi wanted to ask Mataal to stop dancing and get to work. But Mataal smiled at him and went on dancing. He swept the floor with his dancing body and Yogi recognized the song to which he was dancing. One of those songs about Meera's love for Krishna. How the queen Meera was in love with the Lord Krishna and drew the fury of her husband, the lord who wanted her to worship him and no one else.

Mataal smiled through his pain like Meera. Her king was cruel to her and locked her up and made her suffer in every way he could imagine. But Meera knew that.

Kamal Swami loved Mataal. He was one of his favourite boys. The boys joked that Mataal asked the Lotus before going to the bathroom.

'The Lotus checks his wee-wee, makes sure it's stiff with pee,' Bora would say. 'And then tells him—go water the world, my pet.'

Bora could say anything. He was real nasty.

Yogi forgot what he had planned. He stared at Mataal, his body glistening with song. She suffered. She suffered for Krishna, her mischievous blue lover. Her pain was her pride and she smiled at him in her pain and she smiled at Yogi. The prayer hall danced with him. The dead smell of the night had vanished and sunlight streamed past the curtain at the door. Yogi felt he would faint.

Then Kamal Swami walked through the door. 'Boys!'
He said with a smile in his voice. 'Where are the others?'
Mataal stopped dancing as he saw the Lotus. But the
smile didn't go. He was not afraid of anything, not when
he danced.

The music played in Yogi's head. The music of Meera's
cry of pain before her Lord. The music to which Mataal
was dancing in silence. He dared not think of Mataal's
letter but it creaked and spread like a cancerous map in
his soul. The long letter he had written to Sanket Tudu,
the tribal footballer who looked like a statue carved out
of black marble. It was the letter of a devotee, and yet he
wanted to do things to Sanket's body that nobody had ever
heard or thought about. A long letter written on crinkly,
fragrant paper.

Kamal Swami pulled out one of the rolled-up carpets.
Swiftly, he rolled them out on the floor. His saffron robe
rippled in the air.

He opened the cupboard, took out a pack of incense
sticks. He struck a match and lit them. Smoke blew out,
thick and fragrant.

Two other boys in the prayer hall team walked in.
Sleepy and a little annoyed. But they saw the Lotus and
stood erect.

'Flowers!' The Swami exclaimed. 'Where are the
flowers? Still not here?'

Nobody said anything. The gardener was late some
days. Nobody cared. They just packed them around the
shrine quickly. Sometimes a garland hung limp from a
corner of a photo. Kamal Swami always came closer and

took care, placing a fresh garland around the portrait. He missed nothing.

'Come with me,' he told Yogi. 'I'll send the flowers along.'

Yogi stepped out. The music wafted out with him. *The more you loved him the more you suffered.*

All her life she had suffered. Old age brought no respite.

The Lotus walked fast. Sometimes it was hard to keep up with him. The sun was still mild outside. Birds chirped.

'She loved Krishna all her life,' he told the Swami, softly.

'I know,' he said without looking at Yogi. 'The Lord waits for such devotees.'

'She had a sad life.'

'Those who love him truly suffer. Pain is their mark of honor.'

They entered his room. A room of cream white walls. Soft smell of incense. A small temple.

The Swami stepped into the room and turned to him. The door was open and Yogi looked inside. He had been inside before. Many times. There was nothing; a small bed, just about enough for one person to stretch out; a small writing desk. A light saffron sheet covered the bed. It was the closet of a temple. Not a speck of dust anywhere.

'I would like to enter the order.' Yogi said breathlessly.

The Lotus laughed. For a moment Yogi felt a mane of wild hair sweep across his fair and green face. But how could it? His head was shaved like all other monks. But there was a halo of sweat and sunlight. He had beautiful white teeth but one. There was one tooth in the middle of the bottom row that was deep brown. As if he used to chew paan in the past. Yogi had never seen that kind of laughter. Like a child's. A happy child's laughter.

'Ask yourself.' The Lotus said, kind eyes looking at him. 'It's time for many hard questions. So many.'

Yogi looked up to him, a bird with pouted beaks.

'Can you let go of the world?' The Lotus asked. 'Like that?'

Yogi stood still. He wanted to nod but felt frozen. What was there in the world but dust and noise and cigarette smoke? He wanted to get away.

'Does Kajol know?' The Swami asked softly. 'Have you spoken to him?'

Yogi felt a sudden jolt. Kajol would be there, naturally. How could Kajol not be there? Kajol would always be there, everywhere. But he had not said anything to Kajol. Would Kajol hate him for it? Would he get mad? He had not thought about that at all.

'I love how you leave your mind,' Kajol always said. 'How you just step out of it, like a shirt. Yogi. A real Yogi.'

To be a Yogi, one had to step out of one's mind as well as one's shirt. Did Kajol like him shirtless, mindless?

What would Kajol say if he became a monk? Shirtless, mindless, robed in saffron? Would Kajol still like to touch him, play with his fingers? Yogi couldn't think about it anymore.

'I have decided.'

The Lotus reached out, touched his shoulder.

'Think about it, be careful what you want.' He said. 'If you give up the world you cannot go back.'

The Swami's palm was light on his shoulder. The fingers were callused but soft. Would the fingers move? Would he caress him?

It had been a long time. Since the day he had shown him how to blow a conch.

Shonabitch

Thursday afternoon's event left the boys in Bliss Hall feeling naked.

The girl was younger than them. If she went to school, she would be in Class 6, maybe 7. But children in Mosulgaon didn't go to school. They wandered into the ashram through the cracks in the wall and gathered dry leaves and bits of wood and thrown away plastic bottles and cookie tins the boys got from home and sneaked out with the loot.

The girl had gathered an armful of trash when the sky began to roar. It was past noon and the blinding sky turned dark and wrinkled into spurts of lightning. Blue-white sparks that wriggled and split open the black clouds. The boys shuddered even to step out on the balconies. This was the time set for shower before they went down for lunch and then back to school for the second half. But the girl didn't look up and went on picking at the trash-heap near the Hall.

The sky cracked into a torrent and the girl was trapped under the ledge of Charity Hall right opposite them. Now she kept frowning at the sky, perhaps worried that she would lose her trash in the flood.

Nobody knew Kamal Swami would come prowling. He was usually in school at this time. Maybe the rains had made him change his plan. He walked straight into the row of Class 9 boys pasted straight along the corridor, at least twenty of them—shirtless boys in bathing shorts staring at the rain. They stood along the long arm of the 'L' of Bliss Hall, trapped inside the grills of the ground floor corridor like a knot of caged animals, staring at the ledge of Charity Hall that faced them.

The girl had dropped her pile of garbage and hugged herself tight. It hit like a lightning bolt that she was wearing so little. A loose shirt, perhaps the top of a salwar-kameez or a grown man's kurta and nothing below. It was so soiled and tattered that it was hard to say. The rain had plastered the kameez around her body and she stood hugging herself, staring at the rain.

The Lotus must have stood there for a long time. He never rushed. Then he called: 'Will looking at the rains make everyone clean?' His voice fell like a whip on their naked backs. 'The dirt won't go even if you're scrubbed for hours under boiling water.'

There was bitter laughter in his voice.

Red welts appeared on their skin quickly as they looked away from the girl under the ledge. Did she see them? The crowd of towel-wrapped boys on the balconies above?

Shame hung over the corridor like a red cloud. They wanted to see the girl, her skin. They were hard and breathless.

Welted by the Swami's words, they lined up for the

bathroom. They did not look out to see if the girl was still there or had fought the rain to go back home.

Suddenly, something was lost.

A beautiful passage was read out during prayer that evening. A passage about women and gold, drugs that ambushed you on the way to god. Women were gold; and gold, women. They cast a spell on you.

It was a beautiful passage read out by Niraj Bora. Why did Kamal Swami make Bora read this? For him it was a pain, stammering and stuttering and all that. Continuous reading in Bangla lay many traps for him, perhaps continuous reading in any language. But as he read, the prayer hall gasped with the wet dreams he proudly shared in the hostel, about the bodies of the mothers and sisters of his classmates, dreams that had caught like wildfire and made Bora the big boy in Bliss Hall.

The red cloud spread in the air again, the redness and the beads of sweat on Bora's forehead as he trudged through sentences about the drug of women.

Yogi did not dare to look back, for the fear of Kamal Swami's closed eyes, the smile dancing across his mouth like a white cloud on a sunny day.

At dinner, Kamal Swami announced that they were going on a trip that weekend to a beautiful place— Chandrachur, the moon-mountain, a town by the Ganges where the monastic order had its headquarter. Just a few hours from the ashram. A blessing of a place.

'Whoever goes there,' the Swami said. 'comes back a changed person.'

Saturday morning was a riot. They piled into two giant tourist buses. All of Class 9 was going. One hundred and twenty students. Sections A, C and E in one bus, and sections B, D, F in another. English and Bengali medium, mixed up.

Kajol had entered the bus early and got a seat by the window. He had saved the aisle seat for Yogi.

'Changed person, perhaps,' Kajol said. 'But it's still a waste of the weekend.'

To be able to sit next to Kajol made Yogi happy. But there was also a rash of fear. Kajol had his goal sharp and clear. He had signed up for coaching for the engineering entrance exams, Sylvan Mentoring. Once every month, they sent whole question banks of Class 12 math and physics and chemistry reprogrammed in mind-altering permutations. Kajol knew the questions they would mail every month and the four years till Class 12 were just a waste of time as he was prepared to crack the IIT entrance tests already. He was on his way and he was going to take Yogi with him. He would do nothing without Yogi.

'Why?' Yogi had asked. 'Isn't this nice?'

'The half-yearly exams are just around the corner.' Kajol had frowned. He looked like a little boy when he did that. 'I wanted to get started this weekend. Especially on the trigonometry.'

'Trigonometry?' Yogi was terrified. Did they have trigonometry? In Class 9? He couldn't ask.

He averted Kajol's glance and looked down. They were

wearing their school uniform. Ashen shorts and white shirts made of coarse cotton. It had to be the cheapest kind of cloth. Even though the saffron worn by the monks were smoother and shinier and the great secretary-monk wore saffron silk. The over-starched coarse cloth clung to Kajol's dark and thin legs like a sheet of paper. His legs were almost hairless and there was something insect-like about them, the bulbous knees, but right beneath them Yogi could see the tiny blisters like permanent goose pimples and for some reason he wanted to scratch that skin very gently.

'Why are you always with Sushant Kane?' Kajol frowned. A jolt shot through Yogi. What was he to say?

'He's a good teacher.' He said weakly.

'He's a bad guy.' Kajol looked outside on the speeding road and rested his arms on the armrest between them. His bony elbow touched Yogi's arm.

'He smokes ganja in his room.'

Only bidis, Yogi wanted to say. But he didn't know if he could say that. So he kept quiet.

'You haven't spoken much to him, have you?' he asked. 'Outside class?'

'I don't have time to waste.' Kajol said while looking out of the window. His upper lip throbbed like a bird's wing, quivering as it fought against the wind. He was unreachable. So brilliant, so angry.

'I know he fills your head with nonsense.' Suddenly Kajol turned to him, grasped his wrist. 'Seriously Yogi, get back.' What would he do with his wrist? How long would he hold on to Yogi?

The boys were chatting and laughing and somebody was singing at the back. But they were all far from them. Nobody looked at them.

'What?' Yogi felt a twinge of shame as soon as he uttered it.

'It's Class 9!' Kajol looked straight at him. 'Do you have a goal in life?'

Yogi rested his hand lightly on Kajol's.

Kajol pulled his hand away. 'You can forget about getting Science in your Plus 2 if you score below 90 per cent in your boards.'

I can never be as good as you, Kajol. He wanted to say. *My handwriting will never be as beautiful as yours.*

'And then what will you do?' Rage sparkled in his eyes. 'Take the IIT entrance test from the Commerce stream?'

'I don't care about the IIT, Kajol.' Yogi said.

'Of course, you don't. It's only your life, why should you care? When you can lock yourself in a room with a shady man and smoke ganja?'

Yogi felt throttled. Kajol always did this to him. Where were they going? What did the future hold?

He was going to say something nasty when he heard the roar.

'Apples? Grapes? Strawberries? Apples, did you say?'

Mihir Dam, the PT teacher, was wobbling his way along the aisle of the bus like a drunkard. Always the first thing he said when his temper exploded. *Apples. Red juicy apples.*

'Your father buys you apples? Apples from Kashmir? Hundred rupees a kilo?'

Guppy was Ankur Banerjee, large and round with the complexion of Europeans. He had pink patches on his huge cheeks that became red when he was flustered or terrified. As they did now. His parents worshipped him and loved to brag about what a fancy cricketer he was and how highly prized in the snazzy cricket clubs of Calcutta like at CCFC and the snooty cricket camps. Guppy's family was as rich as they looked and both his parents were some corporate bigshots. But that didn't explain why their cricketing IQ was subzero as Guppy barely lasted at the wicket for a ball or two after wielding his pricey English Willow like a giant spoon a couple of times.

Guppy was the kind of boy Mihir Dam loved to beat into pulp.

'So your father's a rich man, is he?' Mihir Dam shouted hoarsely. 'He feeds you apples, does he?'

Do you eat apples? Mihir Dam screamed this question whenever he attacked a boy. Short, dark and square, he was a poor villager who had won the blessing of the order and made a living as one of the sports teachers at the ashram. He knew deep down that boys made mischief for one reason, and one reason only: their fathers' money, and the pride that came with it.

The driver drove faster and faster. He was terrified of the scuffle at the back. Mihir Dam pulled Guppy by his hair and banged his clenched fist on his back. It was like an explosion. Even on Guppy's soft, cushiony fat. After all, he was right about Guppy.

The fat idiot couldn't hold a bat to save his life but would not stop bragging about the pricey cricketing gear his parents had gifted him. Especially the bat, apparently real English Willow, that cost a bomb. He wished he could take it to the town of Chandrachur where the temple courtyard would be the perfect place for a match. He also said something about rustic old fogeys who taught the boys sports but wouldn't know a piece of English Willow if it hit them in their face. He had said it loudly when the bus had stopped by some empty field where the driver wanted to take a leak. He was stupid that way.

There was something sad about watching Guppy being thrashed. Because he was a clumsy and helpless boy, so fat that he took two seats anywhere. And his parents certainly never touched him except to kiss and coddle him so being hit was an unreal thing; his body didn't know which way to shake and tremble and he was too zapped to cry. But it was also kind of beautiful because Mihir Dam kept shouting about apples and Guppy looked, well…like an apple himself. Large and pale with reddish cheeks that got redder and redder the harder he was hit.

'Now he will burst,' said Bora, transfixed at the violence.

Mihir Dam turned to him as if electrocuted.

'My father is a farmer.' Bora said like a robot.

Luckily for him, Mihir Dam turned back to Guppy. He slapped him on his cheek. There would be short and stubby finger marks on those pale cheeks for a few days now.

Yogi glanced at Kajol. He was looking out of the window. He liked to pretend such things never happened.

Yogi had never been to a place like Chandrachur. It was quiet and saffron and breezy and merged into the river that flowed past. The air smelled different. It was pure and full of faith and you felt someone was smiling at you all the time, someone who cradled you in his arms high above the dirt of the world. You also felt that this person had glasses and the kindest smile in the whole universe. When you thought about it there were happy monks in billowy saffron robes, many of them wearing glasses, rushing from one house to another, talking to knots of people, sweeping the steps and watering the trees.

The boys marched in a clumsy antlike procession, rows of white shirts and ashen trousers, elbows and black shoes shooting out in odd directions. It felt fine in school where they belonged but here the huge temples and monasteries and prayer halls were large and wide open to the world and there were people from all over, tangles of white foreigners milling around and the river flowing away forever.

They walked the boys through the rooms where the Happy Bearded One had spent his last days, rooms full of dark wood and white cotton sheets and large wrinkled cushions and Yogi felt he could live there forever. It was like living in a prayer hall. They showed them the field where the twelve original disciples of the Happy Bearded One had gathered after his death one wintry night and had sworn over smoldering log fire to pledge to the brotherhood.

Yogi smelled the river as they walked through the ashram. The Ganga. It was a river the colour of ash and saffron and blue smoke, the river of yoga and burning bodies and hymns and snow that came down from the mountains up north. It took in everything, flowers and leaves in prayer, human waste and charred belly-buttons from corpses burnt at the crematoria that dotted its banks, even the smoke of factory-chimneys, and sang along its way to the sea. Out here she spoke Bangla and cradled the ashram town of Chandrachur and covered it lovingly with a sandy hue.

There was no real sand but the temples looked sandy. It was sand the colour of the robes the monks wore. Sometimes they were aflame, deep and amber, almost a shade of orange. Then they looked intense and angry, like they were on fire. But more often they were faded, a kind of light dusty saffron that looked old and peaceful, the kind that faced the world with the childlike smile of a happy old man. They looked old but if one looked closely they were beautifully crafted and nothing was chipped or broken or mossy like real old temples. The main shrine looked like something a talented child had put together after traveling around the world. There were pillars like those in ancient South Indian temples and steeples like churches in Italy and domes like mosques in North Africa along with brickwork that looked like terracotta burnt and shaped in the villages of Bengal.

They had lunch in a long hall with the coolness of a mud-thatched roof, sitting on long benches with long tables before them, just like the dining hall back in school. It felt cooler here as they were on a holiday and there was no need to rush through lunch to get ready for the rest of the school day. And they were being served! Brahmacharis only a few years older than them served them rice and dal and fish caught from the river. The Brahmacharis were monks-in-waiting; boys who had vowed to enter the order but were serving the twelve-year apprenticeship before they earned their saffron robes. They wore white robes and the colour looked boyish on them but also a little stupid. They had their eyes drowned in the dal they served and refused to look up. But a couple of them smiled at the boys and asked them to eat well.

Later in the afternoon they sat on the grounds where the twelve monks had gathered before a log fire after the death of their guru. Now it was a field with manicured grass. But there were two banyan trees that were over a hundred years old, so they must have been there when the Happy Bearded One died. It must have been a strange and bare time. They were poor young boys who had left their families and taken the mantra from the Happy Bearded One, Himself touched with the madness of God. They burned their guru, came back from the crematorium and discarded their clothes, shaved their heads. Then they put on the saffron robes and picked up their alms bowls and walking sticks. They promised to live by begging, wear nothing but the robes of the monk, the wooden flip-flops as those used by gods in exile.

Standing there, Anirvan felt liquid electricity shoot through his body, scarring his flesh. There was something, something to be done in life. Something that would rage in the world.

Flames had danced on their faces as they joined twelve hands to pledge eternal brotherhood, for earthly life and beyond. They had nothing but their begging bowls. And yet they were the richest young men that the motherland had ever seen.

They would carve her sleeping dream. The nation of saffron.

They were to sleep in a giant hall. On one massive bed. They had rolled out dozens of ribbed carpets and spread swathes of white cotton sheets over them. It was hard and there were no pillows. But Mihir Dam told them that they could sleep with their arms under their heads. The soft part of their forearm made a nice pillow and the posture was also good for the spine. A few boys had brought air-pillows they planned to inflate after the lights were out. The monks would not allow it.

It was exciting to sleep there. It was hard to say why. The place looked like the school assembly hall where they gathered to say their prayers. *To truth from untruth. Take us. To light from darkness.* Also a bit like the room where wedding guests spent the night of the wedding with the newlyweds, singing and laughing and gossiping. Perhaps it was the white sheets. The wedding hall also had white sheets spread all over, with long-stemmed roses wrapped in silver foil everywhere, the red petals torn and scattered at the end of the night of merrymaking. But the white sheets on the wedding bed always looked crumpled, even before anyone sat on them. Everything in the assembly hall was clean and straight and taut.

Kamal Swami came to inspect the hall. They sat quietly while he walked around, his soft clean feet treading the white sheets on which they were to sleep. He looked around, his face hard to read—the mouth parted faintly to reveal two small uneven teeth but it wasn't a smile. He was checking to see if they were quiet and well-behaved; also perhaps to make sure everything was okay and no boy had to sleep on the floor.

But things had become tense even before the Lotus entered the hall. It was Tavi, he could never control himself. The boys had dumped their knapsacks on the spots where they planned to sleep. The usual knots had formed. The problem was that someone had dumped his knapsack next to Rajeev's. Once someone did that, it was sacred as the place was 'taken.' But Tavi wanted to sleep next to Rajeev, and when Tavi wanted something that looked hard to get, his upper lip quickly became dotted with sweat and he started to stammer. It was frightening because when these things happened Tavi could do anything—he became a kind of demon, totally different from the laughing left arm fast bowler who decimated the opponent's wickets at every third delivery and cheered with his teammates.

But today it was scary as it was Lothar who had dropped his knapsack next to Rajeev and had 'booked' his place. Not that Lothar cared where he slept, he had probably dropped it by accident, but it was not good for Tavi to fling his knapsack away and ask him to scoot as the place next to Rajeev was, naturally, his. Rajeev looked worried but playfully so, as he was friends with both Tavi and Lothar. But Lothar looked up with bloodshot eyes and said something that had a nasty American slang in it, which made things worse as Tavi, who was from the Bengali medium, did not know much about American slangs, just enough to realize when something stinky was being thrown in his face.

But Kamal Swami walked in right then and the fight had to be flung under the sheet. The sheet stirred like a wounded animal. Everybody sat quietly as the Lotus glided through the room and eyed every inch and the light shone on his shaved head. In their corner Lothar's eyes grew redder and redder like they had dead flies in them and Tavi stammered to himself darkly and tightened and loosened his right fist ceaselessly. Yogi leaned closer to him and heard a word repeated like a mantra. 'Shonabitch.' It was Lothar's fault really, he spoke too fast and faster when he was flinging some mean street curse and now it was up to Tavi to sit and repeat what he had heard like a mantra till it made sense to him but it never would.

Kamal Swami barely said anything during inspection. They all wished he would say more, perhaps grumble a bit or be mean in a salty, pointed way like some of the other monks. 'Is that your underwear or a turd? Smells like it.' 'Next time you walk in with your shoes I'll make you lick the floor you haramzadah son-of-hell.' Some of the monks spat things like that at the boys. The Lotus was clean and quiet but his eyes roved behind his shining glasses and the boys' hearts beat fast and faster. Their skin crawled with shame and the air felt heavy. Why did Tavi, the big and loud fast bowler, want to sleep next to Rajeev who seemed to care about nothing and was always singing holy songs in his girlish voice? Why, everyone knew why he did. But who would talk about it but in a whisper?

Whose fault was it? Tavi's, for flinging Lothar's knapsack away or Lothar's, for refusing to move from Rajeev's side? It was a done thing that Tavi would sit next to Rajeev in class and the prayer hall and the study hall and so it was natural that he would sleep next to him. Lothar had broken that pact and suddenly Tavi's anger looked like a naked animal that panted and gasped with a sweaty upper lip. He *had* to sleep next to Rajeev. He would kill if he couldn't.

Yogi looked at Kajol, halfway across the room from him but along the same wall. He wanted to sleep next to Kajol. He wished Kamal Swami had told them how to sleep. He would let Yogi and Kajol sleep together. Would he have? Yogi wondered why he thought that. Yes he would. Kamal Swami understood everything. If only he could sleep next to Kajol. If the day had gone well, they could have planned it. It would be the most natural thing to do, to walk towards their corner of the bed. They had sat together in the bus. If only they hadn't had that fight. They had gone in different directions and had not looked at each other throughout the day. Till now he had not realized how much he wanted to sleep next to Kajol. He wanted it so much that he felt like crying. Kajol now acted as if he didn't care who was next to him. His bit of the bed was clean and the sheet taut, his small knapsack folded neatly across so as to become the sweetest pillow ever. His left arm a shade over his eyes, the smooth skin of his upper arm naked below the tiny sleeve of his t-shirt. But he didn't look at anybody. They would turn the lights off and it wouldn't matter which way he looked or if he looked anywhere at all.

Yogi wanted to sleep with his face nuzzled into the back of Kajol's neck. He knew what he wanted. He would lick Kajol's skin softly but he would wait till they put out the lights. He knew Kajol would lie quietly today, say nothing, not even turn to him. When it was dark, Yogi would sneak his hand inside his pants, caress his smooth bottom, nuzzle his penis against the soft, naked flesh. Kajol would say nothing but perhaps his body would breathe again.

Yogi looked at Kajol. Suddenly Kajol glanced in Yogi's direction but turned his eyes away as soon as their eyes met.

He folded and re-folded his knapsack. He pretended not to notice the fear that hung in the air, the fear of wanting something too much.

Supermen

It was exciting to walk out of the ashram gate. The guards did not try to stop them. They saluted sharply. Yogi knew that they really saluted Sushant Kane but he and Rajeev were also there with him, so they also kind of saluted them, right?

To be able to walk out of the main gate on a school day felt like magic. The only time they walked through this gate was when they left for home during vacations, when the campus was a carnival with parents and luggage and cars and pretty mothers and sisters and the shouts and the chatter and the empty hostels laughing silently behind them. Everything was lovely and lit up. But these days the older boys sneaked out through the narrow alley-strip that ran past the stadium and led to the main road from where they could hail auto-rickshaws to Tejpur where they could buy paratha and beef curry for less than a hundred rupees. Chicken was expensive and most people here from Mosulgaon and the other villages ate beef which felt kind of dusty and leathery but was okay since they were so hungry all the time. But this was past the real huge front gate of the ashram, past the hawkers' stalls and the auto-rickshaw stand and the bus stop, under the colossal bronze swan on the arch of the gate.

Sushant Kane called a taxi and slipped in next to the driver. Yogi and Rajeev sat in the back which was nice as both of them got window seats. The taxi rolled along. It was a strange feeling. They had walked out of the high walls of the ashram in their school uniform and now they were on their way to Calcutta. To a debate competition at a very important place, the Library and Cultural Centre run by the Mission. They were special and so the ashram had blessed them and let them out in the world where they would represent their school to fight for the trophy named after the Great Saffron One who held great crowds in a spell with his words.

The taxi glided along the street past markets, construction sites and makeshift stalls and got on the bridge that linked it to the city. It was a small bridge but it took a long, long time to cross it as it was always choked with traffic. This was the only way to enter the city from the southern districts and all traffic had to pass through it and got tied up in a knot. Beyond it was the city of Calcutta. Hungrily, they looked out of the windows and stared at the milling crowd of vendors, porters and beggars and hangers-on. They had pulled down the windows so that air thick with burnt petrol wafted inside and they breathed in it deeply. The city was here.

In the city, the taxi slowed down. It was a slow fight through the road swarming with buses and rickshaws and wheeled carts piled high with wares from the markets that clogged the road. So many people.

The taxi had stopped. The driver muttered something and took out a bidi and a packet of matches.

Suddenly, Sushant Kane spoke hoarsely. 'Is there a lack of smoke anywhere in the world? Do you have to dirty the car as well?'

'What?' The driver asked, bewildered.

'There are two kids at the back. Spare them the smoke.'

That felt strange. Sushant Kane smoked before Yogi. It was odd to hear him protest against dirty air. SrK was so restless these days, nervous and angry at the same time.

The car slid a bit more smoothly after it left market-infested Garia. It moved through Baghajatin where the houses looked cheap and dusty, even though they were newly made and there were scaffoldings and unfinished paint-jobs. The city was expanding to these parts and this was a housing colony where families of East Bengal immigrants lived. Even after all these decades after partition they liked to cluster together in these new colonies and shout and scream in their savage language. Ivy Kar lived here with her family. Yogi had gone in there once with his father. There were trees and ponds and nobody could understand a word of what they said. Why were these colonies part of the city? They were disgusting.

But after that came nice and clean Jodhpur Park and everything felt okay, and then the streets widened again and it was beautiful to stare at the bridges and the huge billboards and the rows of electronics and clothing shops. Suddenly, the people looked small and scattered and ridiculous. Everything was bigger than them.

The taxi stopped when the palace came into sight. It was a palace. A huge house shaped like a palace and crenellated like a temple with the insignia of the Mission on the top—the lotus in full bloom. This was the Mission's famous cultural centre. The door was huge, like a fortress, with shiny silver knobs on them. There was something royal about the place, and something scary. It was ready to war with the streets outside. Something shot through Yogi. One could change the world here.

The driver buzzed away after Sushant Kane paid him. They walked towards the golden fortress.

There was a small group around a chaat stall on the pavement, restless like a cloud of flies. Three or four of them. They stared at the boys in wonder.

'Yes, look carefully,' a young man pointed at Yogi and Rajeev, his face dark with gloom. 'Those two boys.'

'The season's cut of clothes.' The young man said with a flourish. 'Diaper-pants for hairy boys.'

Yogi's ears turned so red that he felt they would burst. They made a picture—ashen half-pants made of coarse cotton, flapping like cheap flags around legs that looked grown up and naked. Big Class 9 legs. The ashram wanted simple, coarse clothes and they didn't care how the boys looked in them as long as they all looked the same. But now they were out in the city and there were giant billboards around them and young men stared at them with a spark in their eyes.

Suddenly, a wet lizard slithered under Yogi's shirt. There was a girl in the group. She was laughing so hard that she was gasping for breath. 'The juveniles of Alipore jail,' Yogi heard one guy say.

'Seriously, guys,' the first young man continued in his gloomy voice. 'Autumn fashion is here. Take note!'

Sushant Kane softly placed a hand on Yogi's back, but there was a smile under his sharp beard. He could be cruel sometimes.

Yogi ran towards the metalled door of the fortress. Rajeev slithered along like a shamed mouse.

Yogi's breathing calmed as he stepped indoors. It *was* the ashram, the long hallways with marble floors and dark wood banisters and bookshelves with rows and rows of dark brown volumes but everything was well-lit with the late afternoon sunlight streaming in through glass windows everywhere. People walked silently, barefoot after leaving their shoes in the hallways and sprinkling their hands with Ganga water. But it was also a place in the real world and there were men and women in ties and saris checking books out of the library and talking with the monks who were robed in saffron as usual but seemed at ease with this world, joking with it. There were several white foreigners too and the monks spoke to them as if they had not come from faraway but had just sprouted on the sidewalks of south Calcutta like everybody else there.

Sushant Kane breezed through the corridors and the hallways like he was home and it suddenly struck Yogi how well he belonged here. This was the city and the world and foreign visitors and important people came here all the time and right outside was one of the main crossings of south Calcutta full of cars and billboards.

And yet it was also the quiet world of the ashram where people walked without shoes and sprinkled Ganga water on their hands, and where Sushant Kane belonged in the end with his brothers. Somehow they met here.

Sushant Kane took them to the heart of the shrine. The secretary-monk of the Centre sat there with two tall white women. The room was lined with bookshelves along the wall and smelled of fresh incense. The secretary-monk raised a blessing palm and smiled but went on dictating something which one of the women noted down. Yogi had never seen someone like him, not even at the ashram.

His saffron robe shimmered around him and on the writing desk. It was silk. He wore 10 rings, one for each finger. They had different kinds of stones on them, big and small and of different colours. He also wore a cap like Nehru, but it was saffron.

Kamal Swami was just a boy from the neighbourhood streets. This monk *was* the ashram.

Yogi already knew his face even though he had never seen him before. He knew the face from newspapers and TV and countless brochures and leaflets and posters. State leaders came to see him and on special days like the birthday of the Great Saffron One he spoke from every television everywhere.

He finished dictating and turned to them. He spoke to them in a tone Yogi had never heard in the ashram, like they were foreign dignitaries themselves, little foreign dignitaries who had come to visit the centre. He was waiting to hear them debate and he was excited as they were the best of their school.

The moment had come. Yogi would break into the world. Whatever it took.

Sometimes Yogi had the fear that the boys from the Calcutta schools were getting to see things they didn't. They were afloat on birdsong and greenery while the city students were watching news shows on TV and watching adults fight. It worried him during debate and quiz competitions as knowledge of the world spiked the winning edge at these times.

Especially with a subject like 'Winning back the nation'. Most of the debaters spoke a lot about freedom fighters and blood spilled on the streets and the slaughter of the Partition but most of all they spoke about the Great Saffron one who said that the nation would be nothing without its women and how playing football was essential to the nation's health. Everybody knew that speaking about the Great Saffron One would get them more points with the judges here.

Some of them were very smart or had smart fathers and teachers so Yogi heard things like the budget and five-year plans also but he realized that all of them were speaking in different varieties of the military style. That was Sushant Kane's term—the military style, or sometimes the ocean-desert-mountain style where you debated like you were fighting the elements.

Rajeev went up. He spoke like he sang. His thing was all about love and it was heartfelt. That's who he was.

He couldn't go long without breaking into song, and whenever he sang he touched whoever was around. Grab their hand, play with their fingers, throw an arm around their shoulder. He would win the nation back with love.

The guy who went up after Rajeev was from one of the new schools in the outskirts. New-money Schools, Sushant Kane liked to say. He spoke in Bangla but he was clearly Hindi-speaking. Yogi wondered why he didn't speak in English. His speech sounded comical, as he was trying to say things about which he understood nothing. But his voice grew like sunrise. He cared about what he was saying. Whether or not they understood him did not seem to matter so much. Yogi forgot that he was speaking in Bangla. It was like he was speaking in Hindi and he staked his life on it, even though he went on speaking in his kind of Bangla. The hall was in a spell.

It was Yogi's turn. He didn't know what to say. Everything he had prepared withered away like torn clothes.

The story that needed to be said knew everything. The story knew everything.

'We were angry,' he told them.

'We wanted to break things, smash everything the people had. The people who had made us angry.'

The secretary-monk was seated in the front. Along with the judges. He was not a judge. The judges had his blessing.

'We were angry because they didn't let us watch TV. We did push-ups through the evening, and now we could eat the world. We wanted to win India back from the killing fields of Pakistan but they wouldn't let us. We were powerless. We woke up in the morning to run circles around the field, but we ran in circles all day, eat and pray in the prison, study in a blindfold. Then they pulled us away from the cricketing fields of Pakistan while the village outside our walls burst a string of crackers every time India lost a wicket. How could they do that?'

The judges fidgeted. One of them looked like he would like to leave, go to the bathroom. The secretary-monk had his eyes fixed on Yogi. There was a smiling light in his eyes, as if everything depended on him.

'We finished mounds and mounds of rice,' he said. 'We wanted them to feel poor and powerless. To become us. To make them understand that they couldn't feed the boys they wanted to teach the lessons of life. And that would happen through the strength in our bowels. When we couldn't eat any more, we just threw the rice away. We piled our plates high with rice, walked out of the dining hall, and threw the rice down the drain like it had been served to us by untouchables. When all their food was destroyed, their walls would come down and the shiny bald heads of the monks would drip with the sweat of fear.'

Sharply, Yogi glanced at the saffron Nehru cap on the secretary-monk's head.

'It was simple,' he said. 'Just ask the dining hall boys to pile our plates high with rice and then walk out of the

hall, to the long washbasin, dump the rice into the gutter
behind it. The rice looked like a cloud of white flowers
in the drain that was torn and scattered by the stream.
Some of us sneaked back with empty plates and sat at
the tables again and asked for more rice. They were cruel
to us. It was a nerve-destroying match on TV and the
Pakistani bowlers were out for blood. And the brutes in
the village outside shrieked every time the bowlers drew
blood. So we had shrieked back at the Pakistani bowlers
and called them by their true names and the bald tyrant
of the house had just turned the TV off, thrown us out
of the room. It was their great pleasure to take away our
only pleasure. They didn't care about the nation and they
didn't care that the brutes from the village wanted to see
it go up in flames.'

One of the judges got up and edged his way out of
his row. The secretary-monk smiled into Yogi's eyes. He
had leaned forward. Saffron shimmered around him like
a king's robe. Everything else looked colourless.

Yogi did not want to look at Sushant Kane but caught
him through the corner of his eye. He looked at Yogi, his
face unreadable.

'I went out three times, dumped three plates of rice
down the drain,' he said. 'Who wanted their food, these
saffron anti-nationals?'

'In the chaos of the dining room,' he went on, 'nobody
noticed the boys. Nobody who would stop us. We were all
in it and wove a web through the hall. Our friends served
us daal and vegetables too. We threw everything down
the drain. More and more and more. We had to destroy

all the rice in the kitchen before the bald devil came in. Down-the-drain. Down-with-Pakistan. And then,' Yogi's voice crumpled, 'I went out with my friend with a plate sky-high with fresh-cooked rice and the little boy from the next village walked in to wash our dirty dishes and while we flung the rice down the drain and he stood frozen. "So much rice!" the little boy gasped. "You throw away?"

'It was as if the little boy had slapped me,' Yogi said. 'The little boy wore torn khaki pants—ones we had thrown away. He was probably eight years old. He came past the wall to work in the ashram for which he got two meals a day. Otherwise he would eat once in two days. The little boy looked at us in awe. Like we were supermen. We went back to our rooms. Our heads felt heavy. Everybody came and saw the boy frozen near the drain, looking at the rice as if he couldn't believe it. Someone tried to make a joke. Something about the rice being good for the plants. But no one laughed. The rice we had thrown away could keep the village well-fed for a couple of days. The village that burst crackers whenever India lost.'

Yogi looked up. Many people had left for the bathroom. His voice softened.

'That's how we won our nation back—from ourselves. We were awkward, from that day on—before Pir. The boy who had stared at the rice. Pir, yes. That was the little boy's name.'

The boy from new-money school won the first prize. How could he not? No one had left to take a leak during his speech.

Rajeev won the second prize. Love was magical. They didn't have to return empty handed.

The third prize went to one of those boys who tried so hard to sound like a news-show host. Budget and parliament, all such things he spoke about. Nobody understood anything he said, so he had to be given a prize.

The secretary-monk came and clasped Yogi's hands. He had not taken his eyes off him. Ever since Yogi had started speaking. Surely that was not possible. But it felt that way. His clasp felt like a hug, something which swallowed Yogi's whole body and pressed him against the saffron silk.

'My son,' he said in a musical voice, 'you've won your nation back.'

Sushant Kane waited till the great monk had vanished with his train of little monks and polite white devotees.

'Well!' Was all he said.

Delight coursed through Yogi. SrK's face was all lit up. Suddenly he realized that praise from this man meant more to him than all other praise in the world put together.

Next to him was the same man. From the dark restaurant in Tejpur where they ate beef and paratha. The large man who had mocked Yogi.

His eyes glowed.

'Let's go,' he said.

There was a light in SrK's eyes.

Acharya

His name was Raghav Acharya. He was a friend of Sushant Kane.

He looked like he had been a sportsman in the past, maybe a football player. Now flab had grown around his body, and yet he had a touch of the wild.

Quickly, he guided them out of the palace, into the city air. The shiny metaled door closed behind them.

Rajeev had left with his mother. She had come to listen to him debate. She was joyful about his prize, grateful to his teacher who had trained her son so beautifully. His speech on love had melted the audience. She had taken him home where he would spend the weekend and come back to the ashram on Sunday evening.

They walked, the three of them. Raghav walked on Yogi's right, and Sushant Kane walked next to Raghav. As if he wanted to keep a little distance. But he walked with Yogi.

'You were fucking with me that day?' Raghav asked, his eyes on the road. 'In Tejpur?'

Yogi did not say anything.

'You knew what you guys really did that night.' He said. 'You knew what all that wasted rice had done to Pir.'

'And still you were fucking with me.' He paused before the sea of traffic.

They had walked to the main crossing at Ballygunj. Roads forked out in several directions here and the traffic was a shrieking mess. It took 15 minutes to cross this place.

Where were they going? Yogi had no idea. Sushant Kane wouldn't say anything. But they had a plan, he knew that.

'Today, you sounded like you knew what it's like to starve,' suddenly Raghav looked at Yogi.

Raghav held his hand and shot through rows of moving cars like a cat and suddenly they were on the island in the middle. For a second Yogi sensed what he might have been like on the football field.

'I know you don't. But you can sound like you do.'

And then the same thing again. Like an invisible arrow, Sushant Kane had also reached the other side. Next to them was the big Kwality restaurant with its dark glass door before its air-conditioned interior.

'That's kind of incredible.' Raghav stood on the pavement. 'A fucking dangerous kind of incredible.'

'Now you need to see,' Raghav said. They walked into the noisy side street.

'We don't have much time,' Sushant Kane said. 'I have to take the boy back to the ashram.'

Raghav raised an arm. *Wait*. Like a traffic cop stalling a car.

Sushant Kane walked steadily on the far right, smoking a cigarette.

'You need to see,' said Raghav, walking along.

'Yes,' Sushant Kane spoke in a muffled voice. 'Yes, Raghav, yes!'

Raghav said nothing but kept walking.

They arrived at the train tracks. The street seemed to end there. People clotted around the place; they had tried to build homes there. Muddles of clothes were hung over wicker fences and green froth oozed through cooking pots on small fires. The people looked exhausted; the women leaned against one another and chatted, poking the green froth from time to time and the scattered children squealed like birds and animals.

'Sit down,' Raghav said and sat down himself right on the tracks. These were rusted tracks where no train had run for ages.

Yogi looked at Sushant Kane. SrK held out his handkerchief. A clean white handkerchief. 'Spread it out and sit on it.' He said softly.

'This is a lot like Pir's village,' Raghav said. 'But much worse. No rich ashram next door that they can climb through the walls for odd jobs. And the city's a killer.'

'The rice you guys threw away that night would have started a riot here.'

Yogi kept quiet.

'See what they are cooking?' He pointed to a frothy pot. 'The children fight with the cats and the dogs all day at the local market to scavenge throwaway bits. Vegetable skin, fish gills, stems and roots and bones. The kids are like dogs.'

A shiver ran through Yogi. He heard the kids squeal and grunt but not say a word. Animals.

'But not getting food is not their biggest problem. They grow fine on gills and tails and throwaway skin.'

'Look at that shop,' he pointed to a shack on the other side with a small clot of people around it.

'That's a country-liquor shop. That's where the men spend most of their time.'

'They find the money to booze even when they are starving. It's killer stuff. Whitens the floor if you spill it.'

He turned to Yogi. A part of Yogi wanted to slink away. He was a big man, with something of the athlete's pure power.

'If you want to talk about poverty, that's the real problem you have to talk about.' He pointed his finger to the shack, his eyes fixed on Yogi. '*That.*'

A hand touched Yogi's shoulder. Sushant Kane had come and stood next to him.

'We need to go back to the ashram today.' He said slowly.

'The streets,' Raghav whispered. 'The real place to tell stories. Not air-conditioned halls of posh schools.'

Gently, SrK pulled at Yogi's hand. Yogi followed him. But Raghav, Yogi realized, would not let him go.

The Lotus Skin

The question buzzed inside Yogi's head like a fly. Why was Sushant Kane so quiet that Friday afternoon? Even on the way back to the hostel. There were just the two of them in the taxi, but he had barely said anything. He had just muttered something about the traffic bottleneck on the bridge at Garia. Yogi did not know what to say.

Chat. Have a conversation. SrK liked to say. A speech is a conversation with many people at the same time. A conversation where everyone feels you are speaking to them alone.

Yogi wanted to talk to the Lotus. He felt like a fool. The Swami knew Yogi in ways that didn't make sense to Yogi. Under his saffron robe, he was a forest of wild green shoots, full of wild, wet energy. He knew Yogi could recite well. He gave him difficult passages to read aloud in the prayer hall and during the school assembly, passages that gave him gooseflesh. But he never said anything about his debating. Neither had Yogi ever seen him speak to Sushant Kane.

There was the Swami and there was Raghav. It did not make any sense. The Swami was here, but just out there was a dark, dusty roadside eatery. The Lotus lived close to leathery meat that was neither chicken nor goat. It was madness.

Yogi walked to his room. The warden's room was the first one in the ground floor of the hostel. The curtains were drawn. Heavy saffron curtains that sat still.

He drifted into a familiar fragrance: sandalwood and flower and incense and a soft yellow orange sheen all over the room. But there was someone else in the room. She sat on the chair across Kamal Swami's study table. The Swami sat at his usual place.

She looked at Yogi sharply as he entered and he knew he hadn't seen anyone quite like her here at the ashram. She was probably his mother's age but had the eyes of a young college student, eyes which searched the room keenly. She wore a cream silk sari that looked expensive but one which was borderless like that of a widow. Yogi smelled camphor and something else, something beautiful and pointed, like clove. He stood still at the door.

'*Kire*, what is it?' Kamal Swami smiled at Yogi. His cheek creased with the familiar smile and a deep happiness drifted back to Yogi.

'I...I,' Yogi tried to say something but the smiling eyes of the woman made him freeze.

'Just wait outside,' the Lotus smiled again. 'I'll call you.'

Yogi stepped out and stood behind the curtain.

'There was something in that voice,' the woman's voice floated through the curtain. 'She always said, that made her want to give up everything in the world.'

'He was a lion of a man,' the Swami said in a smiling voice. 'But she too was special, to be able to hear his call.'

'And follow him till the end of the universe.' She responded.

'Helena was a very special woman.' He said. 'How many people of her birth and wealth feel that their calling is with the world's poor?'

'But how could she say no to that voice? Did she have a choice? That bronze skin and those deep eyes? Just look.'

Her eyes, Yogi knew, had stopped at the giant portrait of the Great Saffron One on the wall of Kamal Swami's room.

The Lotus didn't say anything. Was he smiling?

'Tell me Swami,' her voice softened. 'Was that all for her?'

'Men like him come to the earth for just one reason,' the Lotus also spoke in a softer voice.

'I know,' she said. 'She was a miracle woman. A goddess hailing from Parisian high society and making India's poverty her own. But would she have come here if she didn't love him?'

'She loved. There was so much love in her heart.'

The curtains brushed Yogi's cheeks. There was another kind of music in there. Kamal Swami's voice was like a conductor's hand; the beautiful woman's voice rose and fell as the Swami's voice asked, as if the Swami was telling her how to talk, and how to feel.

But her words fought him off.

'But when a woman hears your voice and looks into your eyes and decides to turn her life upside down, a man must know something, doesn't he? You know, don't you?'

Her voice shivered.

'If I touch you,' her voice softened. 'Like this. And this and this, tell me,' she asked. 'Don't you know?'

'I know all there is to know,' Kamal Swami's beautiful voice boomed and Yogi longed to see his smile. 'He was a man but in form. He was but the Great Spirit.'

'The form too, feels, does it not? Tell me it does.' The woman paused, as if taking a deep breath. 'Is it true? Is it true that once while they were traveling together, just the two of them, she had…'

'No, Helena!' Suddenly Kamal Swami's voice became warm. 'He had said, reminding her of her great calling on earth right then. Never forget why you've arrived in this world. Never!'

'No?' She sounded almost hurt. But strangely, Yogi felt if he could see her face he would see her smile.

'No,' he said. Yogi couldn't help but part the curtain, look inside. The woman's hand lay on Kamal Swami's palm like a dead branch. 'Gold and women. Women and gold. They cannot touch the brotherhood.'

He had never seen Kamal Swami smile like that. Never like that. He felt a sharp ache, as if the bones inside his chest had shifted suddenly. He knew nothing about the Lotus.

He turned and walked back to his room.

The Poison Bowl

'These people belong to us,' Raghav said as the auto-rickshaw started to crawl through the housing colony.

This place always left Yogi desolate, with the mourning sound of wind over empty land. It didn't seem fit for human life. The houses were half-born, with bits of wicker poking out and plaster unfinished on facades, and there were ponds half-covered with swathes of water-hyacinths.

'That's a strange thing to say,' Sushant Kane said.

'Where would they go?' Raghav asked. 'They are not the rich of Calcutta who vote for the Congress. They've been with us ever since we gave them the land on which they were squatting after they came to India. What did the Congress do except throw them out of their homes?'

'Really, Raghav?' Sushant Kane frowned. 'Is that what your Party says? Seems a bit extreme to blame the Congress for the Partition of India, no?'

There was loving laughter in his voice. The two men shared something that Yogi couldn't quite figure out. Something they didn't talk about but which still glued them to each other. What was it? Yogi tried to touch it every time he saw the two of them together. He couldn't make sense of the language. But he had realized that it was about believing in the same things.

They lived different lives. But Raghav seemed closer to Sushant Kane than his own brothers. Looking at them together, Yogi knew why Sushant Kane never seemed happy in the ashram where his brothers belonged. And yet he had to live there. That was his real family. But he didn't believe them.

Was that why he always brought Yogi here? But he was always making fun of Raghav, poking holes at everything Raghav said. And yet, when Raghav reached out for Yogi, SrK's eyes sparkled. As if he knew something he wouldn't talk about. What did he want Yogi to do? Yogi ached to know.

'They still live like refugees,' Raghav said. 'People in Calcutta make fun of their language. They belong to the poor people's party. They always have.'

'Brothers and sisters,' the thin boyish man seated next to the driver spoke into the hand-held loudspeaker. 'Go around your house carefully. Look everywhere. In the bathroom, the kitchen, outside under the shed. The bowl of poison is closer than you think.'

'What is he talking about?' Yogi asked, startled.

'Love!' Raghav said mysteriously. 'Pure love.'

'Pure poison.' Sushant Kane snorted.

'The bowl of poison,' the man removed the funnel-like loudspeaker from his mouth and paused for a second, returning quickly. 'The nursery of killers. Go around and look for them. Please, please do. Brothers and sisters, for my sake.'

'Doesn't work as well as it used to,' Raghav looked past Yogi, at Sushant Kane. 'You guys are just mad,' Sushant Kane took a drag at his bidi and laughed. 'No wonder they call it blasting a canon to kill a mosquito.' 'Bowls of accumulated water,' the man turned and winked at Sushant Kane. 'Sitting still. Breeding ground for the killer babies.' He spoke with a flourish, almost breaking into song. 'Malarial mosquitoes.'

The singing auto-rickshaw hobbled over unformed roads past homes that looked like half-cooked tea-stalls, giant bamboo scaffoldings for construction that looked abandoned, houses with their jagged brick facades covered with clothing spread out to dry—men's cotton underpants flapping over windows and rust-coloured saris winding around the houses like unfolding stories.

The man recited a string of details like a long poem he had memorized. Blood tests, a charitable dispensary, the state health department, fever and symptoms of malaria. He was so thin. Yogi marveled at the burst of energy that carried his words through the air and worried that the man might collapse from the force of his own words.

'Flush the still-water out of your lives and let it flow,' the man sang. 'God forbid the poison enters your lives and you meet malaria in person. But if you do, you know what to do and where to go.'

Sushant Kane flicked his cigarette-butt away. 'Here comes the best part,' he said.

'The charitable dispensary sponsored by your well-wisher and councilor, Raghav Acharya, is forever open for you.' The man screamed. 'At all hours of the day and night. You are welcome, forever welcome!'

The auto-rickshaw took a turn and hobbled past a pond. At the end of the pond was a field with tall wild grass and a single goal post.

'Brothers and sisters,' the man took a deep breath and screamed. 'Go around your house carefully.'

Suddenly Yogi wanted to laugh. But he couldn't. Something about this made him ache inside.

'The market makes slaves of everybody,' Raghav said. 'Why go for something free when you can pay for it?'

'Is that so?' Sushant Kane said. 'Don't people queue up for freebies?'

'Not true. The crowd's thinning out these days at the dispensary. There's a new clinic near the market where they have a female receptionist—not a compounder but a receptionist. And they charge a fee. And they are all going there to find out if they have malaria in their blood.'

'They actually want to pay?' Sushant Kane asked in a slow voice.

'It's not a lot of money,' Raghav stared absently at a cycle-rickshaw far ahead of them. 'Twenty rupees. But if there is a fee, it must be good!' He said mockingly.

'Not that he needs the money,' he spat. 'The booze keeps him well-oiled.'

'Ratul Munshi?' Sushant Kane asked. 'Ethyl Alcohol? He owns the clinic?'

'Who else?' Raghav gestured to the rickshaw, now right before them.

A shiny cloth poster flapped on the back of the

rickshaw now right next to them like a gown trailing behind the vehicle. On it, a plump tri-colour palm blessed all and the smiling face of a balding man with a neat wisp of a moustache stared at them, wavering in the breeze. *Vote for Ratul Munshi.* The words rippled like an oceanic wave as the poster flapped in the wind.

'He helps them with the loans they owe the banks for their rickshaws,' Raghav said. 'And with parts, maintenance, help for the families. In return they have to flap his face on their ass.'

'The rickshaws with the white chadors have taken over these parts.' He said as they passed the rickshaw. 'Ratul smiles at us everywhere.'

'They are putting serious money into the campaign,' Sushant Kane said.

'Of course,' Raghav said. 'Ratul has his own mint. The IMFL chain shops. Cows that never stop giving milk.'

'IMF?' Yogi asked, sharply recognizing something from the news shows.

Sushant Kane ran a palm through his hair. 'Indian Made Foreign Liquor.' He laughed. 'Scotch brewed on the Highlands of Karnataka. The International Monetary Fund will never figure it out.'

There was a dark delight in Sushant Kane's laughter. What had happened? Raghav and Sushant Kane had a secret language, private jokes to which their bodies swayed.

'Keep everybody drowsy,' Raghav said bitterly. 'And then fling a silk chador with your face on it over everybody's heads. Dumb heads.'

The auto-rickshaw approached the offices of the Communist Party of India (Marxist) near the main road. They could see a knot of Raghav's men around a carrom board.

'Everybody lives in a stupor of alcohol these days.' Raghav whispered. 'Fog over their brains. Remember the slums across the railway tracks?' Suddenly, he turned to Yogi. His eyes burnt bright.

'That's the vile stuff, killer hooch,' Sushant Kane said and Yogi saw pale fire in his eyes. 'Something terrible might happen one day.'

'Something might,' Raghav muttered. 'One day.'

A smile shone in his eyes, a splinter of glass in sunlight.

The auto-rickshaw made a dying noise and stuttered to a stop. The driver waited as the thin boyish man got down with his loudspeaker.

'I'll do the evening rounds.' The man looked at Raghav hesitantly. 'There's the blood donation camp, and then I'll get directly into the campaign.'

'Doesn't matter what you do,' Raghav said bitterly. 'Doesn't matter what you say. Our voices are dying here.'

Like lightning, he turned to Yogi. 'Will you speak for us?' He repeated feverishly. 'Will you?'

A shiver ran through Yogi. He looked at Sushant Kane.

SrK was looking at Yogi. His eyes were those of a little boy who wanted something but was afraid to ask.

But he was quiet.

You craft a speech when you talk to many people at the same time. When you can make everybody feel you are talking only to them. No one else.

Speech would belong to Yogi. Finally.

Yogi looked at SrK again. SrK's gaunt face glistened with sweat.

'I've heard you speak,' Raghav whispered. 'I know you believe in us.'

'He's young, Raghav.' SrK whispered. 'He's very young.'

'People will listen to his voice,' Raghav said, unmoved. 'They will believe in him because he believes in himself.' 'We have a terrific youth wing,' he went on. 'They do great work in the neighbourhoods.'

'We have to be careful,' SrK said softly. 'Those are college students. He's much younger!'

'We need him,' Raghav said, trancelike. 'Young blood. The things such young blood can do.'

'But who will I speak to?' Weakly, Yogi asked.

'To small groups in these neighbourhood.' Raghav spoke in a voice of quiet assurance. 'We'll tell you everything.'

He could? He could, really?

Yogi would do it. Would that make SrK happy? That's what he really wanted, didn't he?

He would just have to talk to a few people. Not many people showed up at these meetings these days, the auto-rickshaw screamer had said.

Raghav wanted him to do it. He had faith.

'We will train you,' Raghav said. 'Every afternoon in my office. Vacations are coming.'

Yogi nodded.

'Come and see us work,' Raghav's voice softened. 'Everything will fall into place.'

SrK didn't speak. Gratitude was quiet on his face.

Breathless

The Puja vacations came crashing on them. They were all supposed to go back home for a month. The hostel would be closed.

Yogi didn't want to go back home. It was a dark and damp hole. He wanted to stay in a sunlit world. Could he stay back in the hostel? He told Sushant Kane. He would understand.

'Come and stay in our home,' SrK said. 'Will help your studies too.'

That was what Yogi told his parents. They both seemed relieved. His studies would improve if he spent the vacations in the teachers' quarter. They didn't want to question it.

But how was he going to tell Kajol? Kajol would never understand.

When he heard it, Kajol's delicate mouth was bruised with acid.

'You've lost your mind,' he said calmly.

'Why are you so mad?' Yogi wanted to ask. But he couldn't gather the courage.

Kajol stopped speaking to him.

He just refused. In the presence of others, he pretended Yogi wasn't there.

No one else knew anything.

Kajol had become angrier and angrier with Yogi over the last year. Studies and exams were hurtful subjects that never led to happy endings. And Yogi was always gone! Kajol knew. That Yogi had been secretly leaving the ashram with Sushant Kane during the afternoons to vanish for hours. Yogi never told him where and Kajol wouldn't ask. Whenever he came back, Kajol would look away, pretending he didn't exist.

Kajol hated Sushant Kane. He hated everything about him: the trimmed beard and the perky verse and the sharp words.

Yogi wasn't sure when Kajol started hating Sushant Kane. Perhaps after he saw Yogi spend more and more time with him. Kajol wanted to own Yogi, own and shape his life. No one else was real.

Yogi tried to talk to Kajol. Kajol came back early from the games, as if he couldn't break out of the habit. This was usually when they walked up together to the rooms, either his or Yogi's. They chatted. Kajol nagged Yogi about his habit of shirking football and wasting his time at the Central Library. It all felt like small talk. Both their hearts beat wildly because they knew it was time for their evening shower and the hostel was still empty.

But Kajol wasn't speaking to Yogi. He said nothing when Yogi entered his room. He was back, sweaty from football and he took off his t-shirt, which he would wash carefully while showering. Yogi liked to look at his lean and small body. It was dark and shiny with sweat. Sometimes Yogi joked with him and punched him lightly on his upper arm. This felt like an acceptable way of initiating touch; the touch became softer, longer, lingering, every time. Quickly they would lose themselves in each other's bodies but never letting go of that extra pairs of eyes on their backs in case anyone caught them. The darker bathroom was a safer place. In the light of the room, Yogi sometimes felt reluctant to take off his shirt before Kajol as his body was neither sweaty nor well-built. His skin was fair and delicate and his body was un-athletic, too thin and unformed. This was when he wished he was better in sports.

Yogi tried to talk. Kajol had just taken off his t-shirt and anxiety had started to thicken in the room.

'It's just the vacation,' Yogi said. 'Why are you getting so upset?'

'You've lost it!' Kajol flung his t-shirt away in the corner with sudden force. 'Don't you get it? You're going to throw the vacation away, I know.'

'And what is it that I should do?' Yogi felt a lightning flash of anger sear through him. 'It's the *vacation*!'

'Vacation!' Kajol shouted. 'What are vacations for? You're in Class 9 and you pretend to know nothing!'

'Stop telling me what to do,' Yogi's voice hardened as he spoke. 'I can't live the life you've planned for yourself.'

'It's the life of sensible people.'

'What is the point, Kajol?' Yogi looked at him calmly. 'I'll never be as good as you. I will never get the same IIT ranking as you, hell I'll never get into the same place as you and then what do you think is going to happen? You'll go off somewhere and break records and make new ones and I'll be studying commerce in a small city college.'

Kajol looked at Yogi, stunned.

'We'll grow up and go away with our lives.' Yogi said. 'We won't live in the same hostel forever.'

They would go away. The real world was breathing on their necks. Yogi was already there. This world was an illusion. A childhood dream.

Kajol picked up the t-shirt he had flung away. He looked ashamed that he had flung it away.

'You are a fool,' his voice throbbed with tears. 'A stinking fool.'

Yogi reached out and touched his shoulder. Kajol was crying. Suddenly, somebody ripped off the top of Yogi's heart and left it burning in the raw air.

Kajol wanted to mold him. He wanted him for all his life and didn't want to let go.

But he couldn't. School would get over and life would start.

Kajol's shoulders were moist with sweat. Yogi's palm wanted to stay there forever.

'Let's go and shower,' Yogi said.

The afternoon light was still strong when they went to the bathroom. It was empty. It would be a while before the rest of the boys came back from the fields.

They turned on two of the showers and stood under them. Kajol's hair was plastered to his scalp and he looked like a little boy. Yogi's heart ached. He wanted to hug Kajol. Kajol's eyes were closed and trembled under the spray of the shower. He opened them. They looked tiny and weak, as if they were afraid to face the world.

Yogi took him in his arms. Kajol closed his eyes. The strong spray of water cut across their skin and it felt as if they were swimming. Under a spell, Yogi lowered his face to Kajol's neck. He kissed him and felt the water run across his lips. He didn't know water could make him so thirsty.

Kajol hugged him tight. But he would not open his eyes, which would not fight the rain. Suddenly, the shower felt warm, very warm. Yogi lowered his face and licked one of his nipples. It was small and brown, with sleepy sprouts of hair around it and tiny crests of gooseflesh awake around them like a garland.

Like a snake, his hand traveled down to Kajol's shorts. His penis was hard and awake and came into Yogi's hand eagerly. Yogi knew how Kajol liked to be touched. Kajol's body had told him, and he had learned easily.

As Yogi pulled the zipper down and held Kajol's penis tenderly in his fingers. He wanted to kneel and take it in his mouth, eat him like food.

Kajol opened his eyes. Suddenly, they shone in yellow horror.

It was as if someone had slapped Yogi. He ran out of the shower stall, sick to his stomach.

He wrapped himself in his towel and shot out of the bathroom. No one was back yet. He shot along the corridor to his room.

Everything was broken.

Yogi didn't want to see him anymore.

It was the easiest trek, from his hostel room to Sushant Kane's flat in the faculty quarters. A cycle-rickshaw was enough for the two suitcases he had. It would take less than 10 minutes.

Yogi passed Sushant Kane's room in the block, number 25. The block was empty—all the boys had left for home. SrK's room was locked but the windows were left open. He paused for a minute. The open windows were dark pits. The windows which drew him outside these walls, three years ago. He looked at the windows. They looked small and childish.

The teachers' quarters were cottages about 10 minutes' rickshaw ride outside the ashram gate. Sushant Kane shared one with his two brothers—Prashant and Ashant. Most of the year nobody lived here as the brothers lived in the hostels with the boys. But they came here sometimes, and spent most of the vacations here.

None of the other brothers were at home, but there were other people in the house.

Sushant Kane had to ring the doorbell several times before Naren Das opened the door looking confused. His hair looked mussed as if somebody had been running their hands through them ceaselessly for the past couple of hours. He looked at Yogi but looked away absently. It was as if Yogi was the newspaper boy or the milkman; there was no surprise at seeing his classmate appear at this strange home.

'Geometry or physics?' Sushant Kane raised his brows and asked.

Naren Das ran his hand absently through his hair

and suddenly, came back to the world. 'There were a few equations,' he laughed shyly. 'Sorry I didn't hear the bell.'

Sushant Kane smiled but didn't say anything more. They walked in. Yogi was puzzled. What was Naren Das doing here? Das was from the Bangla medium, the boy with a tiny face and an athlete's body. He was a beast on the football field. Just a couple of weeks ago he had got into a foaming fight with Lothar during a match. He was also good in studies, especially science and mathematics. But he was from a remote village and was very weak in English.

Another boy had stepped out from one of the rooms. He, too, looked a bit ruffled, as if he had just got up from sleep. Luben Kisku, the tribal boy—a Santal, probably, also a magical sportsman in almost everything imaginable— especially football and running. But poor in studies.

He saw Yogi but said nothing, and quickly slipped back into his room.

Yogi left his suitcases in the room where Naren sat with a hideous frown on his face. Yogi tried not to disturb him and slipped out quickly. Naren sat before a large notebook filled with tiny, beautifully etched equations and a mathematics textbook from Class 12 sat open on the desk. It felt like a study hall in open air.

Sushant Kane brought two cups of tea from the kitchen. He had made the tea himself. Yogi felt a tingle of delight.

'You know the three of us were taken in by the monks,' he said. 'We were orphans.'

He did not say anything about who his parents were.

Yogi knew they were not really orphans. But he knew the story. You could say that they were orphans, after a fashion.

'We've become part of the ashram in our own way,' he continued. 'Prashant, Ashant and I. To each his own.'

'I guess we end up doing what the ashram did to us. In our own way.'

Yogi was under a spell. He was telling him a story, and the story would tell a lot.

'Every vacation a few boys stay in our house,' he said, looking into Yogi's eyes. 'Boys who come from very poor homes, sometimes remote villages. Where they can't study. Going back there is a kind of drowning. Sometimes they come from homes where there is no electricity.'

'Prashant is the one who gets them here.' He said. 'He has his own way of looking at things. He usually brings boys who are good at sports. He gets to know those boys better. Many of these boys are also very poor.' He gestured to the rooms where Naren and Luben were.

'But this is the first time I brought a boy home for the vacation,' he said. 'I had to.'

He smiled, spreading sunlit happiness inside Yogi.

Yogi asked, 'Why did you?'

The phone rang.

'That would be Raghav,' Sushant Kane got up. 'He knows we're supposed to be here by noon.'

He looked at Yogi as he picked up the receiver. His eyes glistened.

Suddenly, Yogi had his answer.

It would just be a homey little chat with a few people who lived around these tracks. Now he knew what Sushant Kane had meant. A conversation with a bunch of people, letting them into the gossip.

He learned. Watching them do their business in Raghav's office. The office mimicked the poor neighbourhood, its windswept desolation. A room of whitewashed walls and uneven bricks that stared and waited for a coating of paint, a carrom board perched on four bamboo poles outside. He was the boy on the corner mattress, a boy who looked like he might be asked to serve tea anytime. He watched them all. The taxi driver who had his license seized for reckless driving and now wanted it back without the penalty of a fine. The barbershop owner who was in trouble with the police because of girls in his shop offering cozy massages to clients. Hawkers who feared their pavement stalls would be bulldozed by the municipality.

He heard them all.

'Sit back and watch,' Raghav said. 'You'll know everything. And then you will tell them.'

They would love to hear from a student—a young person who knew that being in school was important. The slum kids would have someone to whom they would look up. The older boys could see what their lives could become. And the men could see what it meant to think clearly, speak without a slur.

The mothers would love him. They were all tired of seeing the same old faces, hearing the same old voices chanting the same mantras. A fresh young voice would catch their souls.

He watched and learned. His voice shivered but he didn't say anything. Just a handful of people showed up at these meetings. The auto-rickshaw driver had already said so. Torn and tattered people from the slums, strewn around the railway tracks.

Yogi had to tell them a few things.

He had to be gentle, to hold their hands and sway them.

Gold

Raghav's office was a friendly place. It beckoned the streets inside and called people to drop in for a cup of chai. Yogi got used to lazing there, blending with the cheap, flapping calendars and groaning ceiling fans and the stray dog curled up asleep under the chairs, soaking in the sound bites flying in the air.

The three women who came in that afternoon did not look like they trusted the world. They were different. They might have been troubled housewives from the neighbourhood who had come to snitch about firecrackers too loud round the corner. But Yogi knew there was something. Something that said that their lives were tied too close, too tight. As in the rhythm of string puppets. Were they tall members of a co-op market that had run into a snag?

For they were tall, two of them, tall and regal, and a shorter third who looked like their teenage daughter at first glance. Renu caught Yogi's eyes before the rest, perhaps because she was closer to his height, with eyes that darted at him though he'd done his best to quickly look away.

But a strange co-op group it was, bruised by violence

too beastly for language. Suddenly, both Renu and Raghav were teenagers lost in a flow of jagged slang. But Yogi hung on, not daring to blink, afraid of losing their words. 'They enter our rooms as clients,' Renu spoke in a voice laced with calm wrath. 'And beat up our girls. Cigarettes, belts, the works.'

It was a co-op where men walked in to buy women. Sometimes small girls. By the hour, for the night. It was a co-op that needed to run smooth, which sent its key players out in the world to get business sorted with the leaders of the people. Renu grew deeper in years as she laid out the madness of it all. Making his way through the coded language, Yogi saw a mind to which one could not say no.

The wives of their key clients were pulling a cheap trick this time to get their men off the women who took care of them in the evenings.

Bitches. They had rallied themselves into a cranky ring cast around the right party. The party that hated meat. The meat of women that men liked to eat in illegal massage parlors and hotel rooms. Meat set their blood boiling. They rammed down doors with sharp tridents to wrench out the flesh of people who liked to eat.

They had egged those butchers to break up the good work of perky women who picked up hardworking men at the end of a tiring day to give them the free run of a woman's body. Mountains-deserts-oceans. Climb-hike-swim. What would those bitches offer in homes littered with kids? Hardly a tender word, and you could forget about a hike or a swim.

But why would the bitches bear the pain of their men's pleasure? Rough with anger, Renu's face revealed a cruel woman of the world. Gooseflesh stood throbbing on Yogi's skin at the smell of her body—a live whore sitting and talking in the very same room, wicked brilliance reddening the tips of his ears. Hidden under a silken sari, her body swelled with stories to tell and Yogi's heart jumped to his mouth in terror as he glimpsed the smooth, light brown skin of a flat midriff between her blouse and sari.

The rival party had jumped at the chance. Angry women of soot-stained homes made up a bank of votes that rarely reached the polling booths. Here was their chance to win over the women who wanted their men to come home with the money made in the day and not blow it in the bed of some woman who could curl her body like a snake. So why not beat up a few whores? Catch the men with their pants around their ankles, penises drooping faster than they could rise. Make it the house of shriek and shame it was meant to be.

A fly on the wall of that adda, Yogi saw the birth of a glowing thing that evening. A future. Between the two of them, Raghav and Renu opened up a way of thinking that Yogi didn't know existed. The big-boned councilor and the small, doll-like prostitute pushed the limits of what one thought was possible, beyond the mere fighting of goons by goons, muscle with muscle. Pretending to dust furniture and photo frames, Yogi realized the crying need that had hidden itself so well in the air blessed by stale cigarette smoke and Renu's maddening fragrance. The need of a strong collective will of hookers. Not a shriek but a steely voice of demand. *A union of their own.*

'And why not?' Renu creased her brows. 'We run a good house. We give what we promise. We raise our children with care, better than some of those bitches wedlocked by their husbands...'

'But of course.' Raghav hummed. 'Children...' His voice trailed away in the dusty air of the room.

'Yogi,' He had smiled. 'Why don't you come and sit here?' He flouted his own rule with such indifference that Yogi's flesh grew red and warm and he thirsted for a place to hide. *They were to pretend he didn't exist.*

Renu looked up, gave Yogi a smile of such molten warmth that the world turned, in a flash, to a sunnier place. 'Come and sit, little man,' she said, the dark blue anger from a moment ago gone like a nightmare that had never been.

'Some of you have children his age, right?' Raghav asked.

'My daughter would be a couple of years older than him,' one of the tall women said. 'She goes to school too.'

'Yes, many of us do,' Renu said softly. 'I have a son a few years younger than him. He lives with me, watches me work.' Her face darkened. 'Life! What are you going to do?'

'Here's what you are going to do.' Raghav leaned ahead, the old glint of revenge peeping through his tiny, slit-like eyes. 'Talk to the world. Tell them your stories. Claim your rights.' He grabbed Yogi's hand. 'Have him around. He is a boy with a special gift.'

He looked at Yogi with a helpless smile. A smile that
was shielded from the three women, not in body, but in
soul.

He dared Yogi to do it.

A few weeks later, the beast was born.

'Justice for sex workers,' said one orange banner,
the colour same as that announcing local volleyball
tournaments. 'The National Sex Workers' Union.' Said
the cool white banner pinned across the wall behind the
raised platform. That made no sense, Yogi told himself.
What was national, the union or the sex workers? And
what was national about prostitutes and pimps from the
sleepy houses across the railway station getting their anger
knotted together? People! Sometimes, he really didn't
understand them!

There was music, and songs, and poems. Paul Robeson
and all that. The gambit was opened by a fattish, weird-
haired woman in jeans and khadi kurta. She was studying
for a doctorate in London and was a professional hell-
raiser for the cause of prostitutes. It was a cause—she told
the crowd—that had a life of its own, in many corners
of the world, where hookers worked with licenses just
like doctors and chartered accountants. She spoke in a
singsong and from time to time looked like she needed
a chalk and a blackboard. But the pale banner of the
National Sex Workers' Union was all she had behind her.
They were not just some pillow, she said, men clamped

their legs around to masturbate and could throw away when soiled. Her nice analysis of masturbation—repeated a few times—thickened the knot of people before the stage and sent strong murmurs through them. These were, she sang, human beings, women just like those who helped them at banks and stores, who cooked their meals and washed their dishes. Agile women who cleaned their pipes to flush out needs that might have turned them into rapists and murderers. By drawing out the violence, taking it on themselves, these women were like sharp, skilled snake-charmers. *Help them stand up for their rights.* She flung a khadi-wrapped arm in the air, and a fist rolled into a ball.

Oh, and pillows did not spread diseases. Human beings did. Without a sane system and a sprinkling of peace, they would all be wiped off by AIDS.

Shooting little arrows of terror into every man's loins, she stepped down.

Next was the hookers' chorus, a song by a famous dead poet about mountain-climbing. Hiking across endless deserts and swimming through bottomless oceans. All to be done in the dead beat of night.

Then Renu walked up to the stage. She spoke the same way she had spoken in Raghav's adda. The same clear, simple, cutting spray of words, the straight attack at the jugular, the same intimate manner, biting, caressing. To what a crowd! College boys tickled by the colour of the gathering, housewives back from grocery shopping shocked and frozen on the spot, railway coolies unable to tear their eyes away from the protestors. Not that Renu cared. She had a story to tell. A story of horrors. Madamji was right, she said. Could you get away by bashing up the shop-girl who showed you clothes? Would you have the balls to stub out your cigarettes on your housemaid's cheeks? On her bare breasts? Would you? She paused, looking urgent and composed at the same time. *Would you?* Then tell me, why would you do it to the girl who was just there to do business with your body?

Yogi walked up to the stage. He did not believe a word of what Renu said. He didn't have a thing to do with them, with their sad lives on which goons stubbed out cheap cigarettes.

He passed her. Her mouth melted into the smile that gave him deep comfort. 'My little man.' Lightly, she pulled his cheeks as she passed. 'Go tell them.'

Lovingly, he touched the microphone, moistened it with his slow breath.

'I'm a student,' he began, 'at the school out there.' His finger pointed to the horizon behind the crowd.

No one turned back. No one cared about his school. They were thirsty for him.

'Most boys in my class bring nice lunches from home. Sabji and paratha, bread and omelettes, rice and egg curry, noodles. Their tiffin-boxes shine like mirrors. They have superman stickers across their tops. Lunch hour brings shocks and surprises, every day.'

There were blank-eyed, drooling idiots who had to be respected because of the shininess of their tiffin boxes, the deep-fried fragrance of their food.

The shine on the boxes and the fragrance of the food, they knew, in the shadows of their hearts, were shaped by the ladles and scrubs of their mothers at home.

'There are a few ragged kids who never brought shiny tiffin boxes or fragrant food. On a good day, they got street food wrapped in greasy paper, the covers of their notebooks dark with grease. Savoury stuff sharpened by street salt. On worse days, a few rupee notes to thrust at the street vendors outside the school for some spiced junk in a knitted bowl of dried leaves. Good money, some of them bring, good enough to buy pista ice-cream for a whole row of boys. But never ever did you see them with a tiffin box or a home-boiled egg.'

Yogi lowered his eyes, looking at the crowd in front, and not quite.

'It felt very strange when our teacher, a smart woman who loved us all, told us that the mothers who never packed tiffin didn't hate their boys. What? Were we idiots? Was that what we thought? She didn't. These boys with street food wrapped in grease-stained paper just had mothers who had jobs outside home. Just like fathers. In offices, typing letters. In shops, crunching numbers. Sometimes, in other people's homes, watching over growing kids. Bringing money home for food and rent.'

'Just have a chat,' Sushant Kane always said. 'Even if it's five hundred people.' Yogi's eyes became moist for a second but quickly they were dry.

'The thought of moms who didn't have time to think about lunches for their sons,' he told them, 'was fog that messed with our heads. So we cracked a nasty joke across the back of another boy, an idiot from another class whom we saw lunching on sliced bread bought at the store next to the school. Something about bread from that shop being laced with rat poison. We cracked up in laughter. Our teacher came and smiled. She found the joke funny too.

'She smiled and told us that the idiot boy's mother did not love him less. Just that she couldn't stay at home making lunch for her son as she was here teaching us all. We wanted to melt into the darkest cracks on earth. The boy they had whipped with mean laughter was our teacher's son. The smart young woman who loved us all and had taught our fingers and eyes and minds a thousand things to do. Once and for all, a roomful of boys understood the meaning of a woman who worked outside of home. Who couldn't send her son to school with a well-scrubbed tiffin box and well-fried pooris.

'And then we got the blow of our life. A boy in our class came back to school after missing classes for more than a month. A happy boy everybody loved, most of all, our teacher, because he was clever with his fingers and eyes and mind, picking up with thoughtless ease all she had to teach us. He came back to school a broken boy with the news that his mother had been beaten so much at work that he had to stay back home to take care of her.

'A cup of boiling-hot tea had been thrown at her face, leaving her skin scarred for life. Her head had been smashed so hard against the wall that her hair had become sticky with blood. And," Yogi told the crowd, his fingers loosening around the mike, "We didn't even know the boy's mother worked to make a living. As she lay fainted, they had poked glowing cigarettes at her, burning holes through her skin.

'How would we know?' Yogi asked a college boy who

had stopped at the rally for fun. 'We fought with each other to trade food with him at lunch hour. It was hard to believe that home-fried eggplants could taste that good. Or that one could make parathas so magical that they tasted fresh-cooked after three hours inside a tiffin box. What a beautiful tiffin box it was. Old, but old like a house in which families had lived for many, many years. How did a mother like that find time to work at a job and pay for her son's books and school-fees?

'Who would want to kill her? Who would?' Slowly, Yogi moved a little away from the mike. 'You can ask her,' he said softly. Silence had thickened in a dark clump around the rally, faintly bitten off by the whistle of trains taking off from the railway station nearby. 'She is sitting right there.' He turned at an angle from his silent brood of listeners, pointing to the dark tribe of hookers seated to the left of the stage. The beaten up whore was there too, dressed in the finery of bandages and a plaster-coated arm.

She had no children. Sweetly barren, the best kind in her line of work.

Yogi's body had woven a spell out of which it could not claw its way out.

The hookers' choir had been spared the effort of the last protest song. God was generous with small mercies.

That evening saw the birth of a new labour union. The first of its kind in the area. A newborn, solid block of votes for The Party.

The birth-pangs were loud, lovely and cruel. The flurry of songs and sweets and laughter marked a drunken trail all the way back to the burrowed houses across the railways station, where Bollywood songs were already ricocheting off the walls. Mountains, deserts, and oceans had been climbed, hiked and swum across. *Finally.*

Renu picked Yogi up at one end of the narrow corridor ripped apart by the blaring music. Her strength surprised him, and the muscles on her arms like wiry snakes. 'My little man.' Breathlessly, she stuffed a furry sweet into his mouth. 'You are blessed, my sweet, sweet boy.' Her voice was hoarse, as if from a cold, and it took him a few seconds to realize that she'd been crying. 'Today, I feed you to fullness.' Pushing open the door to her room, she had drowned him in a sea of goodies made by the ladies of the house. Laddoos, gulab jamuns, a platter of sweets made with cashews and pistachios, the warm breath of her moist lips.

Up close, her features were sharp and delicate.

He felt her heartbeat of happiness as she crushed him to her chest. Choking on cream-soaked cashews, Yogi's lips mashed themselves against her sharp collarbone. They were real; they reeked of adulthood. Kajol's bony body passed through his senses. It felt half-formed. Tears welled up in his eyes as he licked the hollow of her neck, sucked its way down to the soft crevice on her chest. 'My little man.' She laughed, pulling herself back to unbutton her blouse, revealing pale shoulders and upper arms, smoother than he had imagined human skin could be. Bracing himself, he scooped her firm and fragrant left breast into his palms, licked and bit its puckered areola. Suddenly, he felt he couldn't breathe.

Painfully, he tore himself from her body to stare at it,

the large, proud breasts over the arched stomach, the deep belly-button, the sari worn low on the waist. She shone with deep laughter and her brown nipples glistened with his spit.

Gold and women. Women and gold. The Great Saffron One always said. Kamal Swami had never given in to womengold. His raging muscles and sparkling eyes lived on their own.

He felt sick and the world started to turn. His lips and tongue were caught in a storm that scratched and bruised and chewed her skin. The hollow of her shoulder, the underside of her breasts, smoothly rough. Her toy-like ribcage and the cave of her stomach. He ate her like a beast and choked from her fragrance.

Pushed against the wall, her body shook with laughter, an undulating river. She squeezed his exploding penis in her palm, wrenching the tip between her thumb and forefinger. 'My big little man.' She had whispered. Fingers laced with killer strength.

Helplessly, he had bucked and come in a hot spurt against the taut flesh of her inner thigh. Spent all of a sudden, he'd marveled at his hatred for her, a hatred more like awe.

Like Kajol's body, its memory was half-formed. It tugged at his heart and made it wet.

A Deserted Temple

When did he get comfortable talking to more and more people? Gatherings a bit bigger, and then a bit more? His audience swelled as he moved into Class 10, fracturing his vacations between his parent's home and Sushant Kane's. He would move into SrK's quarter right as vacations began and the boys left the hostel for home; his mother would pick him up sometime and bring him back home, but sometime mother and son would tell each other that the teacher's place was better for his studies and quickly avert their glances so that the conversation was closed. He knew his mother missed him and yet she did not like to see him in the darkening chaos at home.

Here things moved fast. The promise of a mere ten or fifteen people was shattered soon, into a ragged crowd of fifty. Raghav and his boys pushed him towards larger gatherings and Yogi learned to pretend. At seventy or eighty, he could imagine it was a debate auditorium where parents of every student had shown up. The people looked a bit scruffy. But more intense. And then suddenly he was talking to the whole neighbourhood. It was easy enough to be sucked into arguments at street-side tea-stalls. The inner hollows of government schools gave him a fake comfort, except it was full of adults who would be back here on time to cast their vote behind cheap, flapping curtains.

The stretch between Bandelport Station and the refugee colony became his neighbourhood. It was the most crucial chunk of Raghav's constituency.

Sushant Kane watched him. He looked happy, and there was something childlike about his happiness.

The candied knife. Look like the smiling Buddha while twisting their arteries. *Smile and stab and smile.*

There were those who hated him. Drill sergeant Prashant Kane was shocked at his toxic brother. His was a sports camp for the poor boys. To push them past the sloped gate of the board exam. It was his own cult, the running, sweating cult who swore by the Mission. Ashant never brought a boy home but he cheered the same boys. He was also a devil on the field but his devotion to the celibate order was splintered by pangs of desire for sunglasses and motorbikes. But Sushant was a heretic. He wore pajamas and smoked cigarettes right in his hostel room. He would have been a spiky student leader if he could. If only the ashram hadn't breaded, buttered and sheltered him way back when he had nobody. He would spit on the shrines.

But to bring a boy like this home? A snake? He crashed here every school vacation. Didn't he have a home?

Prashant refused even to look at Yogi while he lived in their house. To Yogi's great relief.

Once there was a world of competitions and prizes and certificates. And teachers patting your head and saying nice things. There truly was such a world. It was now a dream.

There were people who were mad enough to think that they had a shot at toppling The Party from the Municipal seats through which they had grown a wild web of roots. That they could get the rustic refugees in the colonies and the dwellers of the slums along the railway tracks to vote outside the colours of The Party. The scattered night-dwellers who slept on rusted tracks, snatching a living when they could by carrying cargo at the giant crater of the railway-station sprawling across the suburb. To change the minds of the trash heap of humanity scattered here.

The prophet to steer them out of the colours of The Party was Ratul Munshi, a man who had made a fortune through a chain of liquor shops scattered throughout the city and some of the satellite towns around it. Those little nooks where men behind bars handed customers newspaper-wrapped bottles of IMFL—Indian Made Foreign Liquor. Director's Special whisky. Old Monk rum. Vodka marked with a range of Russian vices, shipped all the way from factories in Andhra Pradesh. Running the vibrant empire, Ratul was a man who poured money churned off alcohol into the gaping wounds of society. Building schools and hospitals, a temple or two. A formidable man who had been named Ethyl Alcohol by a brain in ferment. Dangerous and flammable, pleasantly narcotic, devotedly applied to healing the cuts and bruises of society. Ill-health, illiteracy, the works. Cuts that could turn gangrenous without the dab of cotton wool soaked in ethanol.

The Party of the Palm, a bunch of limping, beaten strays gathered up for one last growl, couldn't have chosen better. Ethyl Alcohol was a legend in these lanes, only half-visible as a real human being. A man of mythical wealth in a habit of hushing his source for it, the booze stores garlanding the city like tiny islands of pleasure, he was already a law-giver who jostled with The Will of The Party many times. The Party couldn't wedge a foot into his hospitals, not in their advisory boards, and not in their sweepers' unions. To return the favor, The Party had its very own band of middle-aged women with shrill voices and giant bottoms who blamed every disaster, human and natural, on Ratul's liquor stores, lying down en masse in front of as many stores as they could cover, pledging to live on nothing but the slow-burning lard around their waists for days on end. It was one of the most moving sights in the world, enormous women wrapped in coarse cotton saris rolling across the pavements in front of the liquor shops, picketing the shops to protest everything from hit-and-run accidents to high prices to tornadoes. Sometimes they'd refuse even a drop of water.

How can Yogi ever measure his debt to them? The mean mashis who had, over the years, paved smooth roads into people's minds for him to slip inside?

It arrived as a natural disaster that came at the end of a long prayer. Just as Raghav had promised. Even before the night was out, corpses dropped on the streets like felled trees. Big men who could run across the railway platforms with fifty kilos on their back. Small men with bones dried up from years of card and dice games. It had been a regular workday that had ended with the purchase of a glass or a liter pouch of liquor along with green chilies and mustard oil for homes across the shanties. They came knocking at their wicker door, the hooch-vendors on bicycles. Around midnight, the storm started raging through the hutments, the tornado of screams, of seawaves of pain in the throat and chest, the misted eyes. Hardly any women, none of the wives who paid for most of the booze they never drank.

What happened? Who cared? Some mix up with methyl alcohol and pesticide, they heard. Moonshine laced with fire. A raging wildfire. But who cared? Here it was, their chance of a lifetime.

It was not the kind of chance that The Party could throw at the mean mashis rolling in the dust. Yogi spent a couple of hours locked up in Raghav Acharya's living room with a fog of cigarette smoke burning his eyes, six men whispering to him, a brutal gang that made up the big man's brains and brawns. Sushant Kane had gone back home. There was a smell that defined these gatherings, the sweet and pungent stench of whiskey bought incognito at Ethyl Alcohol's megastore by the railway station. Bought and wrapped incognito in old newspapers, delivered to the Party offices faster than the fat mean mashis could turn their bottoms around on the protest grounds in front of the store.

Soft as silk, they said, as gentle as pineapple juice. Not the liquor for the people. Only for the people for whom they vote.

It was the kind of living room that opened straight into the streets. Like the private clinics of some doctors who are too chatty, too kindly to take their jobs seriously, the kind who open up their doors to all in the neighbourhood who want to drop in for a chai and a chat. Stepping out on the steps, Yogi remembered asking:

Have they removed all the bodies?

'Doubt it.' One of the quiet, sulking types had spoken. 'It's chaos out there. Fresh corpses sprouting every few minutes.'

The magic had begun. None of the writhing men were taken to any of Ethyl Alcohol's free clinics, even though the doctors sat there staring at the doors. The Party boys had done the rounds spreading the shocking news that the IVs there were laced with killer alcohol. That they were good places to go if you couldn't bear the pain any longer and wanted to step out of the world right away. Magically, too, none from the stricken families prayed at the roadside shrines and tiny marble temples carved with the generous booze money. The Party boys, though, had nothing to do with that. On the subject of gods, The Party was silent.

Yogi walked into bustee number eight, a child returning to a family scalded by acid. A forest with felled, burnt trees, creepers wound around the burnt stubs, wailing. Women flailing their arms shrieking in pain, grown up women crying like babies, aching their way through birth canals. Frozen in fear, the babies of the slum had stopped crying. Open-mouthed, they stared at their mothers, unsure as to how they might cradle them in their short, stubby arms to comfort them. The Party boys were dancing around, bloated flies over a sea of muck, pulling out bellyaching men by their shoulder-joints, piling them up in their own rickshaws and auto-rickshaws, into long thela-carts, to take away from the nightmare world of Ethyl Alcohol's clinics and their string of Poison IVs.

In that gutter Yogi was a wedge of the moon, shiny and touchable, that touched you in turn with soft fingers and clean nails. He touched an old woman at her wizened elbow, asked her:

Did you drink the moonshine?

Stunned, she paused mid-wail, a massive, sick fish hooked by the angler.

Did you? Yogi asked again. Her head wobbled, left to right and back again.

She had not. The silly old cow.

Disposing of her, he walked ahead, gently picked a silent six-month old off the arms of a wailing mother. Un-stirring, the mother wailed along, an even wail that cared little about the loss of her baby. Yogi moved in and out of their lives like a limb of their own, a pale, unblemished limb that they never owned, just about eating their food (but never quite), playing with their kids (touching them as lightly as possible), offering them a gift hamper of words they felt could be theirs, if only for a moment. *Did he booze?* Holding up the baby, he asked the mother, the skinned animal shrieking in pain under the butcher's knife. 'No. No. No.' Finally there was a touch of novelty in the mum's wails, a shocked rocking to and fro like a scarecrow caught in the wind. Lovingly, Yogi looked at the tiny thing, a large-ish dark brown lizard covered in snot that drew a wave of nausea out of his bowels.

'So he isn't going to die like his father,' Yogi told the crowd. 'Lovely!'

He held him up, the snotgreen, muckbrown piece of flesh like a chicken roasted and skinned. The maelstrom of wails thinned a little, how could they not? Yogi's voice offered them something in the midst of spiked suffering.

'I hope you have shiny plans for him,' he raised his voice. 'To send him to Ratul Munshi's fine school where he could pick up the art and science of boozing.'

There were posh alcohol companies, he told them, which gave its employees booze bonuses, a wad of money with the salary to spend on liquor, a fine shot to sales. And they did, month after month, year after year, till they were biting away larger and larger chunks of their salaries to buy booze, fattening the companies and shriveling their livers at the same time.

'Christian monks and nuns round up your kids for their school in order to swell their own flock of believers and whiskey companies give you money to buy booze from their own shops. What do you get when you sent your kids to a school run by a booze mogul?'

But even if you're god's own gift to the smelly and the downtrodden, a milk-pure child in a gutter of slime, once in a while you stared at the face of an unbeliever.

An unbeliever who was a suspicious creature, a young labourer who did not drink, was alive and healthy, a forehead creased and eyes wrinkled under the blazing sun.

'Ratul Munshi's shops sell foreign alcohol.' He looked at Yogi, a kindly older brother whose question was wrapped in helpless affection. 'Cheap hooch is all that people here can afford.'

Indian made foreign liquor. Yogi was tempted to correct him. *Scotch distilled on the highlands of Karnataka.* But this was no time to play. Yogi shot him a pair of hurt eyes. Deep in his mind, ripostes jostled with each other in a race to pop out first. Truth: *But for the jacked up prices of IMFL, would the craze for Bangla hooch be so careless?* Truth: Convoluted reason didn't belong to a shaken boy who was getting ready for the uphill battle against pimples.

'Dada,' Yogi pleaded with him. 'You live by the rickshaw, don't you? When you come home late at night, you take out the rupee notes from the pleat in your loincloth, don't you? Notes darkened with the sweat of the day?' In his words, Yogi is his wronged younger brother, a boy hesitant to make eye contact with his elders while he speaks. 'If they are whole, tell me, do the soiled notes tucked in a rickshaw-puller's waist fare any less than the crisp bills in the pockets of pressed trousers?'

The kind of logical muddle, Yogi realized, worked well for the muddy tribes. People who make do with grunts will be dazzled easy with a healthy sentence strung together. A healthy sentence rotten inside.

Two of their boys carried a tall old man with bony ribs

out from behind a wicker fence. The man who could have made it to a slightly fancier death toppled over the gutter halfway through his morning shit. Doomed to die now, fly-swathed on the coir-bed of a free clinic, jaws frozen in the grimace of pain from hooch laced with insecticide.

Yogi looked around the sea of dazed women (and a couple of creepy men who didn't drink), taking a deep breath. 'Why do you run to the city to wipe the bottoms of others' kids when the shit dries on the bums of your own children?'

Why, he asked them, do you scrub your breath away at other people's lives and coffee tables when the muck piles up table-high on your own floor? Hang like bats from crowded trains and get groped by perverts to get to fancy houses to live in dark, damp burrows under them? To suck in their crap like human vacuum cleaners and get your guts and lungs tinted with dust and bleach and cusswords that would piss off stray dogs?

For this?

So that you can send money home? So that your men can go hunting for hooch in crinkly plastic packets that once held Mother Dairy Full Fat Milk? Bangla moonshine in bhads of burnt clay? Husbands, brothers, shaking, spittle-mouth fathers who smell of alcohol instead of the life-saving drops they were supposed to swallow? Spindly, gawking boys who steal from their fathers, their Mother Dairy pouches of hooch?

'All the time,' he told them, 'you thought you were commuting to clean the poop off baby bums and toilet bowls was time spent working for one man only: Ratul

Munshi. To him, you didn't miss a payment. Payment for scorching with pesticide the pest-ridden bodies of your husbands and sons. Lice in their heads and tapeworms in their guts. Pesticide laced with moonshine.'

The mothers had stopped wailing, all of them. Frightened by the peace, a few babies shrieked.

Later that afternoon, the hunger-striking mashis looked on sadly as a jagged mob ripped apart Ratul Munshi's megastore by the railway station, not touching a drop of Andhra Scotch that flooded the sunbaked picketing grounds from the crates and crates of bottles smashed across it. Starving before the store for ages, they had sprouted for it a mild affection, a hurt love as that the devout widow comes to nurse for the flute-sporting god who demands from her endless days of fasting. And paper, endless reams of old newsprint, torn, crumpled, balled legions of paper. In Calcutta, when you destroy a liquor shop, you damage more paper than glass. More paper than what you can murder if you vandalize a newsstand. Newspapers aged from a week to a few years, rolled up in a colossal forest to shade the bottle of shame with which you slink away from its steps.

Paper and glass and Karnataka Scotch, murdered en masse by the masses, thankfully, soon after several crates of the best IMFL had been removed to Raghav Acharya's office.

The temple at the end of that alley gave Yogi pause. He

had never seen an abandoned temple before. Not the way he saw Ethyl Alcohol's marbled gift to the neighbourhood that afternoon; bare, naked and empty, but for a dry marigold garland wound around the shrine and a skinny dog asleep across it. A temple vandalized by desertion.

The mood in Raghav's office that evening was like that of Durga Puja. A Big Brother from the city's headquarters dropped by and he pulled Yogi to his chest in an embrace that sucked all air from his lungs. He smelled of cinnamon and menthol cigarettes, and he had tears in his eyes, a heart that bled for the nation. He lifted Yogi's chin up, looked deep into his eyes and showered him with abuse of every kind. That he was a crazy wildhorse, a tropical storm, a Satanic mill that gorged on human flesh. He strangled Yogi with a garland of bloated, cancerous marigolds and then someone hoisted him up on a jagged bed of human arms and balled fists flung in the air. Later they laid out a spread kids dream about: pizza, three kinds of ice-cream, the fanciest kind of chocolate. Chocolates he loved. All the elders of The Party blessed him, marveled at the power of his innocent feminine voice that had castrated the liquor-nawab and had steamrolled his political dreams, forever and ever, brought to shattered shards and tattered sheets his IMFL megastore.

The girl who gave him the chocolates was tall and smooth, with a face to launch a hundred moisturizing lotions. A supple twenty-year-old goddess, one of the

ambitious student leaders in the college where the reigning
union belonged to The Party. Later in the evening as the
festivities got more and more drunken, she whispered,
'Time to get out of here.' Entranced, he followed her to a
room upstairs where she flung him onto an aged sofa, and
without bothering to close the door behind her, sucked
his young neck in the darkness of the room, her saliva
warm and slow-moving on his skin. Intense pain fought
the sudden need to wet his pants, and his heart beat so
fast that he sensed his death was near. Her right hand
crept between his legs and the softest palm closed over his
penis, harder now than when he had the fullest bladder.
Her fingers played him like a musical instrument while he
gasped and fought the fear that she would discover the
wispy hairs that had sprouted along his groins, his source
of shame. 'The magic voice,' she locked eyes with him.
'There's magic yet in heaven and earth not dreamt in your
philosophy.' She had honors in English, and quoted dirty
lines from Jacobean poetry till she took his penis in her
mouth and he had to throw his weight against the wall
to keep straight, the inside of her mouth was so warm
and moist. When she pulled her kameez over her head,
he asked in a shivering whisper if they could turn on the
lights and she snorted with laughter and fumbled with
the switches to bring the room, stacked with paper and
posters and billboards, to a pale yellow light in which the
dark stare of her nipples brought tears to his eyes. Her
hairless body was that of a crafty snake. Stay away from
the seductive gold of women. The Happy Bearded One
used to say in his childish lisp. The womengold.

He remembered the fine hair sprouted around Kajol's nipples and his head felt ripped apart by lightning. As she threw her weight on him and his bony spine, bereft of his white kurta, hit the couch, they rolled up in a ball and over her shiny shoulders he saw the door close slowly on them.

It was in a slip of a conversation a week or so later that he learned that the girl had gained The Party's ticket to run for general secretary of the student union in the next elections.

Malini. There was a lot Malini would teach him later. But that evening, she broke him into pieces.

Pir and Sana wait for him. The Party waits for them to reach voting age. For the neighbourhood to reach full bloom. They keep him real.

They are weed from Mosulgaon, the half-formed settlement for half-humans outside the spotless walls of the ashram. Spotless but for the dirty graffiti carved there by the dusty creatures of the settlement. Where muddy looking women bathed in dirty pools easily seen from the windows of the hostel rooms. The village of angry, savage people who moaned in prayer several times a day.

Pir appeared whenever Raghav was around. Yogi now knew why. Pir was one of the Party boys. He served people tea and brought the paint and glue with which the cadres put the posters together. He too, would grow up, reach voting age one day.

Yogi was shocked when he saw Sana with him. It had

been such a long time since he had seen her, nearly two years. They were in Class 8 when she'd been trapped under a tree in heavy rain, her kameez stuck to her like dripping skin. The Lotus had caught a crowd pasted on the balcony staring at her. Sana was from Mosulgaon and wandered into the ashram often. It seemed that she made a living picking scrap and refuse on the campus.

Pir and Sana were ghosts around the Party. The Party welcomed children like them—from the railroad slums and the refugee colonies and Mosulgaon. Everybody at the ashram thought the people in Mosulgaon were dirty and dangerous. The siren-song of their namaaz floated into the ashram several times during the day and it felt like a nuisance. Now Yogi knew that people in Mosulgaon hated the ashram. The realization clawed across his skin and drew a trace of blood.

There was bad blood between the village and the ashram. Sushant Kane told him all about it. All these were wild lands and poor villages when the visionary monk from the order imagined an ashram here. The village now called Mosulgaon was already here and the poor dirty people there did not want the brave and kind-hearted saffron monks to build schools and training centres for blind boys and dairy and poultry on their lands and put walls around them that the venom of its poor dirty neighbours could not melt. And they did that and kept the poison away but not the crooked music of their prayer song that floated over the walls so many times a day.

Children like Pir and Sana who wandered around all day gathering their meals and growing up on their own

found their way inside the ashram walls too. Pir even
worked at the dining halls of the school hostel washing
dishes and eating there and they all knew he was from
Mosulgaon but it didn't matter because he was so small.
But he looked smaller than he was as he'd never had
enough to eat. Yogi came to know that he could appear
at places no one expected him to and he had heard many
adults speak their minds. People didn't care what they
were saying before him because he was a small boy dressed
up in khaki PT shorts thrown away by some student and
he cleaned the tables of rice and curry stains before laying
fresh plates on them. So he heard people at the ashram
talking about Mosulgaon, and knew the stories told by
Nitai the ancient caretaker about how they had to come
with the great saffron monks with axes and sticks to fight
the local savages and create the ashram like a newborn
baby.

Pir and Sana were electrified by Yogi. It made Yogi
shudder though he stayed strong and showed nothing.
They hated the ashram. But still they shared something
with him because he was from there. After all, their lives
were lived in and around the ashram, in its garbage heaps
and its piles of unwashed dishes and rain-drenched trees.
Probably they loved him more because he had left the
ashram and joined their Party. The Party that fought for
the poor people's land.

They chatted with him and their eyes sparkled when
they did. He was given rich food—pizza, pastries and
biryani—and he shared his food with them as nobody in
the Party would give them such food. They ate hungrily.

They brought him gossip. They knew things like which housewife in the neighbourhoods had fucked which Party member to get her son into a top city school or which member's farts smelled like deep-fried eggs. Things like that.

None of them talked about the ashram. *Ever.* The empty place. The Class 10 boys had all gone home to prepare for their board exams. The younger boys were there, leading their little lives on the campus with the L-shaped hostel buildings and the mango-grove before the school that all three of them knew well. But they never spoke about that place. Sometimes Yogi wanted to ask if they went back to wash dishes in their dining hall or steal a bowl of dal or pick garbage from the campus. He wanted to know. But he never asked.

When he was on the podium to give a speech, Pir and Sana were always in the front row. Their eyes sparkled even before Yogi started to speak.

They sat still while he spoke, but to him it looked like they were dancing.

Ghosts

Prashant Kane's boys left the teachers' quarters soon after the board exams. The anxiety that had knotted around the exam days vanished and the house started to breathe again.

Naren Das had done very well. 100/100 in mathematics, and near-perfect scores in all the science subjects, faltering in English as everybody knew he would, but he would surely get into the science stream in the ashram's Plus 2 division and from there IIT would be a breeze. Luben Kisku had bombed the exam. He was not as smart as Das and he really belonged to the football field. The ashram had large green football fields. But in the end, you could not belong there. You had to belong to algebra, and to the coaching manuals for the engineering entrance exams. Luben was out. They had given him many chances, even a home and he had failed.

'You got 78 per cent,' SrK came and told Yogi, winking.

'78 per cent!' Prashant Kane said, black shock on his face.

It was an okay score for the world outside. In the ashram, where students came out at the top of the charts, it was a mess. Even Prashant Kane's hardy tribal boys scored a full 10 per cent higher and more. Anybody who scored 78 per cent had thrown his life away.

Yogi felt like a laugh. He was surprised that he had bothered to go for the exams at all. SrK might have been disappointed if he had bunked them. After all, he was a teacher.

Yogi stayed on. He knew where he was headed. Finally. Raghav and Sushant Kane would make sure he got there. There were colleges in the city with rich and festering student unions.

He got into Class 11 in a local college where Raghav's boys and girls ruled the union. For people at home, he had stories. That Sushant Kane was his true teacher and he was willing to let him stay with him while he studied at the college next door. His father barely heard what he said. All he wanted to do these days was to be with Ivy Kar, all the time. His mother could not understand why he needed to stay in the ashram staff quarters even though he wasn't going to the college there but one outside. She had learned that he had become a youth volunteer at the Party office and had started speaking at meetings in one of the city neighbourhoods; she was a bit anxious but was pleased that he was getting close to the poor people's party who hated the idle rich.

'SrK is wonderful,' he told his mother. 'He's helped me all through school.'

'He did, did he?' His mother said. 'God knows you need someone to watch over you. Your father doesn't remember he has a son.'

Yogi frowned. He didn't want to talk about home. He

didn't want to think about it. He didn't remember he had a family. Did he?

'It'll be like staying in the hostel,' he said. 'SrK's house is just outside the Mission.'

His mother understood. But he knew she actually pretended to understand as the most important thing was that she didn't want him to be around their home and his father. Of course it was much better for him to stay with a teacher since he was going to a college next door to their house.

Prashant Kane's eyes cut through Yogi whenever he saw him. Why was he still here? When he was no longer a student at the ashram? But he couldn't say anything. Nothing against his younger brother. Prashant was bigger and more muscular and the boys were much more scared of him but he could not make sense of Sushant. He didn't speak much to Sushant and it was clear he didn't like facing him. What could he do to Yogi?

Prashant Kane hated him. So why did he do that thing?

When Yogi returned from college that evening, Prashant Kane was in the drawing room.

Yogi's heart stopped. Kajol sat next to Prashant Kane.

It was that time of the day. Almost quarter to six—10 or 15 minutes of the day that belonged to them. It was their time, their stolen time, before games ended. Quarter to six. Yogi was always in the shower room at that time, and he knew Kajol would come in, ready to join him in the shower stall next to him. Fifteen minutes before the other boys came back to the hostel. Fifteen minutes of the day Yogi would never forget. He would take those minutes to bed at night, long after they were over.

Quarter to six.

Kajol wore the white shirt and trousers that were the uniform of the ashram college. Strangely, he looked younger in them, as if he was trying to play the part of an older boy. How long since Yogi saw him last? He couldn't think.

'Kajol got 94 per cent in his boards,' Prashant Kane said. '100 in Chemistry.'

Kajol looked at Yogi and smiled. He did not seem to have heard Prashant Kane.

'I know, Kajol,' Yogi said. 'I knew you would do well. Everyone knew.'

'We're counting on him to top the IIT entrance test too.' Prashant Kane said. 'Straight into computer science at Kharagpur! He makes us all proud!'

Kajol did not seem to hear anything. He looked at Yogi. His eyes were smiling.

The poison had softened in Prashant Kane's eyes. Yogi knew he wanted to make him feel sad but he was also really proud of Kajol. Everyone was. How could they not?

'How are you?' Kajol asked. 'You don't come to the ashram anymore.'

It wasn't a complaint. It was just a question.

'Yes,' Yogi said. 'It's been a while since I went there.'

More than a year now. Since the day he packed up and left for Sushant Kane's house. Why on earth would he want to go back there? What did the place have?

'Is Sushant here?' Prashant Kane got up. 'I need to find him.'

Neither of them noticed him. He was gone.

Yogi felt nervous. Now there was nobody else. Kajol could be sharp and bitter.

But Kajol just spoke with a smile.

'The old gang misses you,' he said. 'Shome, Rajeev. Nilanjan has started a new magazine. They get it printed from College Street.'

'Really?'

'And there's a new boy from South Point School who's joined Class 11,' his eyes met Yogi's again. 'He's been acing the debate competitions.'

'Really?'

Aditya Som. Yogi had heard about Aditya Som. Prashant Kane loved to say what a great debater he was. Apparently his speeches were laced with old-fashioned curse-words which kicked audiences into shockwaves of laughter.

'He's alright. But nothing like you,' Kajol said, his eyes looking into Yogi's.

Happiness was a bright light inside Yogi's chest. He wanted to say something but couldn't.

Kajol kept talking. Yogi didn't hear anything. But he saw his lips. Lips he had sucked on for long minutes. They moved, as if he was breathing through them. *Alright but nothing like you.* It rang in his head. *Nothing like you.* It went again.

'Prashant da brought you here.' Yogi said. 'That was nice of him.'

'No, not Prashant da,' he said. 'Kamal Swami. He said I should come and see you.'

Silent lightning blazed through Yogi's head. The smell of incense and the fresh clean cotton of saffron robes, the pale and hairy arms and beautiful buck-teeth. The kind smile that lit you up and saw everything inside. The Lotus.

'Kamal Swami,' machine-like, Yogi repeated.

'I needed him to tell me,' Kajol said.

'Why?' Yogi asked.

'I've wanted to come and see you for a long time,' he said. 'But everything has become different.'

What was Yogi to do?

'I was worried the other boys would find it strange,' Kajol said.

The other boys. Shome, Rajeev, Bora. The rest of them.

No one knew Kajol always came back from the playgrounds 15 minutes early. That they were in the shower stalls when there was nobody there.

'When Kamal Swami told me, I knew I could come. He asked me to come with Prashant Kane.'

Prashant Kane was nowhere to be seen. He had left.

'I can't spend my days without you.' Kajol's voice trembled.

'Why did you leave?' He whispered.

His eyes were wet.

'What has happened to you, Yogi? Why did you go away?'

'Go away, Kajol? I'm in a college in the city. School is over.'

'*Why did you leave?*'

For Kajol, life in the ashram would never be over. It was eternal. It was madness.

There was an ache in Yogi's chest. Blood would stain his shirt.

'I loved those days.' Kajol whispered.

'Kajol, we were kids.' His heart beat wildly as he said it. 'It is the past.'

'Is it?' Kajol asked. 'The past? How easily you say that.'

Words flooded through Yogi, but he didn't speak.

He was terrified that his voice would sound hoarse, that he wouldn't be able to call it his own.

Red Ink

The college attic was a scary place. Swords were bunched up there like flowers. Big, rusty swords like sleepy animals.

'Rusty blades are good,' Raghav always said. 'When you ram them into the bastards you know they are going to be real sick.'

And then he laughed. Everybody laughed. Raghav would never ram a sword into someone. He would be very nice to them. And they would vote for him.

But why did they have the swords up there bunched up like deadly flowers?

'Toys for boys,' Malini always made a face when she said it. 'Just hardwired to remember the violence. The Naxal days when the police made them run so they could shoot them in the back.'

'Swords say Partition,' Her deputy Akram would say. 'Most people think of swords and Muslims together. The ghosts of the partition riots.'

'Because your dicks are chopped at the tips?' Malini would ask.

Akram would laugh but Yogi knew he didn't like that joke. But he had to laugh. Malini was the general secretary of the college union.

Malini made everyone nervous. It was hard to understand why at first. She looked like a supermodel. She dressed shabbily because she was in the Party, but she was so stunning that the shabby dress looked even more striking on her. And she was never angry, always joking around. But people who didn't like her said that she could talk a snake into giving up its fangs to her—that she had really done so and now she carried those fangs at the back of her tongue and the things she could do with her tongue! Talk any crowd into following her like a bunch of zombies. They also said she left three top buttons of her coarse dusty-brown kurta unbuttoned while she did that, but people who hate you will say anything.

Malini loved the sound of Yogi's voice. 'The magic voice,' she would say, 'there's magic yet in heaven and earth not heard in dreams anywhere.' She became a scary thing when she said such stuff.

She taught him the language of politics. Marx and materialism and China and Naxalbari. He learned even though he could not understand everything. With Malini one just learned, one couldn't help it.

Not today.

Malini made him teach classes on the Party. In the college. There were professors who were on their side. They stayed back in the canteen drinking tea while union boys and girls went to teach. And they taught what mattered, not useless things like the old shit in Greece and Rome and Akbar's court. Just the tales of Lenin and Mao. Malini pulled all the other union teachers from the forces and wanted Yogi to teach everything. 'There is magic in your voice,' she would say hoarsely, 'Magic in your throat. Go kill them.'

Yogi lost his way to the class today. He didn't know how it happened. He was just going around the canteen. There were voices, many voices, cigarette smoke, songs, and large white flags with red letters on them like dripping blood. But they felt far away and he couldn't hear the voices properly. Even though they were very loud, he couldn't understand a word of what they were saying. There was spiky graffiti on the walls and the pillars that seemed to melt off like dark kajol on people's eyes. He saw a couple of men and women smile and call him; he saw their hands waving but could not hear anything they were saying.

He could not find his way to the classroom. The students were waiting there. Nobody could leave as the boys from the union would be guarding the doors like bulldogs. He couldn't make sense of where the classroom was. He was only going around the grounds and the canteens and the washrooms down here.

He was alone.

No one knew him here. Malini always said she got him like no one else did. But she was too busy with her schemes and alleys around the union and the Party and the corridors of power in the city. She taught him many things. But she never paused to listen.

The voices rose from the canteen again, like tendrils of blue smoke. The most clever boys and girls sat in the canteen. They were too clever to go to class. They sat there all day talking about Cuba and China and Naxalbari and ways of luring poor villagers to pack the meetings at the Brigade Parade Ground. The promise of a meal usually worked, and clever words worked like a dream.

Everybody liked to talk. Nobody liked to listen. It was all about how loud you could be and how sharp your jokes were. It was like a non-stop fighting match that floated on cigarette smoke.

People were scared of Malini because she could whip them and make them bleed with her words. When she walked into the canteen, the voices hushed. People were terrified who she might attack and who would redden and bleed. Nothing to do with the three open buttons of her shabby kurta. Nothing at all.

Raghav could talk. He always sounded slow and sleepy but everyone knew he heard the slightest sound anywhere. His eyes looked bloodshot like an alcoholic's but he had worked forever to take down Ethyl Alcohol and his empire of hooch.

Words and words and words. They were like little daggers people liked to sink in one another's flesh when they were not looking. Nobody saw anybody or listened to others as everything was caught in the wiry claws of smoke. Graffiti bled on the walls and clotted back into the night again.

Why was he here?

He needed to slow down and breathe. He walked into the washroom. Staring at the mirror over the washbasin, he was at a loss. He had forgotten, suddenly, why he had come inside. Why did he step in here? He did not need to pee. The mirror over the washbasin was stained and dirty. Someone had scrawled in red ink: *Bleed the bourgeoisie to death!*

The walls closed in on him. Cobwebs swam closer and tried to muffle him. Patches of cracked plaster grew larger till the room was about to crack into pieces. Graffiti screamed from every inch of space on the walls—there was a whole universe of them, in all shades of violence. Obscenities, carved in smaller, gentler letters on the wood of the doors, moaned out loud and the bite marks of anger shrieked and tried to punch and claw at him.

He shut his eyes. He thought he was going to crash onto the floor. He wanted to sit down.

He heard the shower.

He didn't want to open his eyes but he knew he was in a large, quiet, airy bathroom. Green shoots nuzzled the huge open windows and wild birds sang odd tunes. He didn't want to open his eyes because his mind was slowly going blank. It had already left his body under the shower and was floating away from it like a wisp of air. He watched his body breathe and get beaten down by the sprinkling shower. But he felt nothing.

'You're lost,' the little boy voice came from far away. 'Lost, lost. *Lost.*'

A voice soaked in love and rainwater.

Safe

A bronze swan crested the gate of the ashram. There was no doubt that it was a swan; yet it always reminded Yogi of a smiling serpent. Perhaps it was the long, meandering neck that shone in bronze. Perhaps it was really a python. There was a serpent, they said, that slept inside us. There was only one way of awakening it. Yoga. The kind of yoga that led human souls out of the cycle of karma, into the black hole of nirvana.

The serpent curled up and slept inside people, like an entangled intestine. The final dream of nirvana was to awake the intestine-serpent, let it swallow the whole human being.

He walked inside. It was green, so soft and green. The air felt pure and clear. To his left was the big ashram office. A different kind of an office. It didn't have the sinister, paan-stained grin like government offices in the city. No paan or cigarettes here but swathes of white cotton and blue. Once in a rare while, a saffron swish. Only one or two monks worked here, and they were almost hidden till one walked out, or went from one room to another.

He walked towards the vast ocean of green. It was their playground. He loved the madness of this place.

But some days his game-time was spent hiding from the playground, sneaking into the library, winding along the path that went past the hostels. Two hours when he held his breath, hoping no one caught him not playing.

Many years had passed since he had walked these lanes. Many years? Why, it had not even been two years yet. Why did it feel like many years?

He walked past the school. The swan floated here again, huge and smiling, on the school's forehead. Here it sat on a lotus, the lotus that promised to bloom but did not quite. Smiling, the swan sat on the lotus, as if it was an egg it was trying to warm to life. Right under the façade was their assembly hall where every morning they chanted the prayers that longed to sing the python awake.

He passed the mango orchard on his right. The leafy trees were clustered so thickly together that the orchard felt dark and moist at all times of the day. As if it was raining there silently, all the time.

If he walked straight, he would get to the huge Central Library. He didn't need to go there today. There was no need to hide.

He walked on the trail that snaked past the hostels. L-shaped buildings that crawled with boys who sang and jumped. Little boys. It was almost evening, and moving in and out of the dining hall they looked happily tired. They had played hard on the grassy grounds.

Conscience. Grace. There was Bliss Hall. His home for three years. Was it not?

He entered Bliss Hall. Some of the boys looked at him but most of them didn't. Did he still look like a schoolboy?

They were on their way back from the evening snack in the dining hall. Some of them with towels around their waists and wet hair, walking out of the shower. It was one of those hours on a loose end, those in-between hours when the boys led scattered lives. They were back from the games and had to shower and eat. Then they would go for evening prayer.

He walked to the warden's room. Amber light shone through the saffron curtain. He knocked.

Kamal Swami parted the curtain.

'Come in,' he said.

He looked at Yogi. Smiles always brought the dimple on his cheeks, like a baby's.

Yogi felt numb. A silken, beautiful kind of numb. His body didn't belong to him anymore. The fragrance was numbing. Incense sticks and sandalwood and fresh clean cotton. Smiling saffron and amber. Colours that created home.

Was he crying? He couldn't say.

'Sit,' the Swami pointed to his bed. 'Here.'

Yogi sat on his bed. There was no cushion, just a few cotton sheets folded and stretched across the wood. It felt soft and smooth and clean, just like his saffron robe. He had never touched his bed before.

'Sit,' the Swami said again, and stepped out of the door.

Yogi had never been in his room all alone. It was such a small room. But it was a beautiful room. There was hardly anything in it. A bed, a table and a chair of dark wood. The table-cloth was saffron, a lighter shade, and there were a few books and a notepad. The three of them looked at him from the wall. The Happy Bearded One, the Great Saffron one, and the Melting Mother.

The room was small, neat and fragrant. It hugged Yogi.

Kamal Swami came back. He sat on the chair.

'How've you been?' He asked.

Yogi nodded. He tried to speak but couldn't.

'Sushant is a good man,' he said. 'Good that you're staying with him.'

'Yes,' Yogi said. His voice sounded lifeless.

The curtain rippled and there was a knock at the door.

'Come in,' the Lotus said, his eyes on Yogi.

Kajol stepped inside. Yogi's heart shifted in his chest. Especially to see him in this room. It was home.

'Sit,' Kamal Swami pointed to the bed.

Yogi moved a little to make space for him. Kajol sat on the other end of the bed. The bed creaked faintly. Yogi shivered.

The Lotus sat on the chair.

'Did you eat your evening snack?' He asked Kajol.

'Yes,' Kajol said.

'What did they serve in Bliss today?'

'Muri, coconut slices,' Kajol said. 'Tea.'

'Oh, nice.'

'Did you eat anything?' Kamal Swami looked at Yogi. 'We have bread and butter today. And hot chocolate.'

Butter and brickbat. Back then they used to joke. Slices of bread as thick as their knees and only the fragrance of butter. Butter was expensive. It was hard to tell what the hot chocolate was. Some thin brown trickle with a touch of sugar. *Hot chocolate*!

Yogi wanted to eat bread and butter and hot chocolate. And live in these rooms. Why did he go away?

The bell rung. The bell for prayer.

The Lotus picked up his prayer book from the table. The green book with the sitar on the cover.

'I have to go for prayer,' he said. 'You sit and talk.'

The conch sang. They blew the conch three times before prayer started. One of the tribal boys with strong lungs.

The Lotus paused at the door and turned back.

'A monk's room is a safe place,' he said. 'Stay as long as you like.'

And then he was gone.

They were safe. Here. Nobody could come in. Nobody could see them.

Safe from the world. Safe from life.

The conch sang again. It started sharp and thin and then slowed down, bloated up, like a balloon, crying a song.

The hostel was empty. Everybody was now in the prayer hall.

'Everybody's proud of you,' Yogi looked at Kajol and smiled.

'Yes,' Kajol said. 'I suppose.'

'You're one step closer to IIT now,' Yogi said. 'What you always wanted.'

'IIT,' Kajol said absently.

'I knew you would do it.'

Suddenly, Kajol's eyes twinkled.

'But who's been changing the world?' his lips curled with mischief. 'One neighbourhood at a time?'

'Sure,' Yogi said. 'Go ahead, have your fun!'

'I went to a gathering at the refugee colony,' Kajol said. 'I heard you speak.'

'You did?' Firecrackers burst inside Yogi's chest. 'To hear me?'

'You look calm when you speak,' Kajol said. 'But you're terrifying.'

An old flash of anger shot through Yogi. Between them there was a red ring of hatred. Hatred for the lives they lived.

'Of course you find it terrifying,' he said. 'For you, it should be.'

'You have a good life. All worked out,' he said. 'Computer engineering at IIT. Then the MBA and a job with a multinational. Right?'

Kajol looked at him. Pain spread a dark cloud across his face.

'Right?' Yogi wanted to take him in his arms, squeeze him so hard that it hurt. Hurt him with vengeful cruelty.

He dreamt of deep red welts on Kajol's naked skin. He would caress them, and watch him shiver.

'Then a lovely wife?'

Kajol looked at him with still eyes. Eyes that trembled with rainwater.

Yogi wanted to claw and scratch at his flesh, make him bleed. He had the sharpest words.

And then the music started upstairs. It was so slow and drowsy. The voice of eighty boys coalesced into a large, lazy animal that dragged its own massive weight. Yogi never realized it sounded so slow from outside. *Cutting the ties to this world, I pray to you.* It meandered. *Full of virtues, you transcend all worldly virtue and quality.*

They were smaller, bonier, awkward boys. Suddenly, they were smooth and hairless and their skin hadn't broken out in pimples. They were in Class 6. The ribbed carpet of the prayer hall was home and bed under their bodies and it would give them shelter forever. White flowers were heaped around the shrine and flames flickered on the lamps and the fragrance of incense floated over them like a slow cloud. But the shrine was far away. Right before Yogi was a small, thin boy covered in the fine white cotton of the prayer chador. Yogi could see his dark skin underneath, and the white vest that he wore under it. Yogi wanted to close his eyes and sing but he couldn't take his eyes off the dark skin and the bony ridges of his shoulders. He stared at it. There was nothing else in the world, just this boy.

At long last, he was a Yogi. The Yogi who saw nothing in the world. Just this boy.

Had Kajol moved closer, or had he? On Kamal Swami's clean, austere bed, their knees touched.

Kajol looked into his eyes. For the first time, he didn't look away.

They were safe. It was a monk's room.

They didn't know how their bodies got entangled. They were plants and suddenly they were a forest. Shoots and stems and creepers were entwined, creating dark, moist shadows and the sweaty fragrance of human flesh. Like blind men, they groped each other, felt each other's cheeks, hair, collarbones.

They kissed. They had no sensation anywhere in their bodies except on their mouths.

Everything was food. Lips and tongue and teeth. All of them were hunters. The teeth and the tongue and the lips. Soundlessly, they hunted. Their lips glowed with spit.

Up above, the song floated like a large, drowsy animal. *Cutting the ties to this world, I pray to you.* The metallic percussion danced like a small, mischievous boy.

At the door, saffron curtains fluttered in the breeze.

The World

'We are such a waste of space, are we not?' He clutched the microphone and spoke to the people. 'We cannot read or write. Books are better than us, so much better.'

The people were quiet. So quiet that nobody dared to move in their chairs. One could hear the squeak. Sometimes he hated it. Nobody ever cheered and chanted when he spoke, like they did with other speakers. Raghav, Malini, all of them got balled fists and zindabad. When he spoke the people became a photo still and it seemed nobody breathed. They stared as if he was a ghastly accident. Usually by the time he was done they were crying, but in silence. But they still stared as if he was a blood-streaked mishap.

'They are a Centre of Culture,' Yogi sang. 'None of you can spell "culture". Yogurt has more culture than you.'

'You are nothing but bodies,' he told them. 'You've entered the earth as bodies, and you will rot as bodies. You will leave no mark on paper. You have to be coached to dip your thumbs in ink and leave an impression when real people, people who also have minds, want to take away things from you, such as whatever chipped coins you have. Or whatever garbage heap of land, as they want now.

'They are holy people. Holy saffron people who are beyond bodies. They have built that beautiful mahogany paneled house with glass doors and leather sofas and, and that thing that would never make sense to you—the smell of books. Never.'

Renu stood next to him. This was her hood and her world. He was her boy. She called everybody over whenever the party needed a meeting. And then she propped him up before the mike.

He turned and looked at Renu. He felt short of breath. He looked away quickly. Renu always knew. He didn't want her to see him.

'Loving saints want this land,' he told the people. 'They are so kind that they look away from the dark lives you lead here, soiling it forever. Nothing but bodies, you are, and you give it to whoever gives you money for the evening. You will never know what it is to have a soul. The kind saints, the pure souls, do not hate you for that. They are still willing to take this land on which soulless bodies have lived and fucked and died and after it is theirs they will make it pure. With hymns and songs and the fresh breath of incense and flowers.'

Hymns and flowers. Suddenly his head reeled. He saw the soft white bed strewn with rose petals and smelled the incense. But then he heard the hymn, the chorus of growing voices, a large, lazy animal that dragged its own dripping weight. It was not a white bed but a thick dark-green ribbed carpet and all the flowers were white, jasmine and tuberoses and yellow garlands of marigold drowning the shrine.

He wanted to sit down, cry quietly.

'And once the kind saints have cleansed your dirty home,' he told them, 'they will build another mahogany paneled, glass-door palace with shelves and shelves of books. Can you believe your luck? Books bound in beautiful leather, books with hundreds and thousands of pages, books which are heavier than people. Nobody will remember the smelly mindless bodies that have romped on this soil. There will only be the fragrance of incense, bound volumes and flowers around the shrines of the gods.'

The people stared at him like they were watching a puppet show with lightning. They were animals. He could call them anything and they would still stare, frozen. And then they would cry like dumb beasts.

'But the Party is selfish,' he said. 'They don't want you up in the air, dissolved in nirvana. They don't want books with hefty spines where your stinking shacks are now. They don't want the clean smell of flowers. They want the stench of your clients' body fluids on your bed, your hair and your saris. They want you here.'

He looked at Renu again. Her eyes glistened, as if with sweat. She stared at him as if in a trance. He tried to speak but suddenly he couldn't hear anything. Something fought inside his throat.

Did she frown? He couldn't tell. She looked around, whispered something to her right.

The Party. He thought he said it but still he couldn't hear anything, not even his own voice. He needed to lie down.

The music struck. The podium floated on it and

everyone could see Salman Khan dance, muscles rippling out of every inch of his skin. Someone had turned on the giant speakers behind the podium. The faces blinked and looked around. Two young girls stood up and shook their hips.

Renu came up behind him. She slipped an arm into his. 'Come.'

He leaned on her and walked. When he was with her, he didn't need to walk. She took him along. His weight disappeared into her and she just floated and he floated along with her. She knew where to go. Always.

They walked over to the beer shack. It was a little hole in the wall where the prostitutes stocked alcohol that they bootlegged on dry days. The warm beer was in great demand among desperate college students.

She cupped his face in her hands. Her bangles jingled.

'My boy,' she said. 'What is it?'

He looked up. His tears blurred her face. But it was there. She was there.

'You're dead,' she said. 'I've never seen you dead like this. Tell me.'

He nodded. He didn't want to talk.

She ran her fingers through his hair, parting them gently. Neatly, she settled them.

'Forget about the meeting,' she said. 'Let's go home.'

He nodded again. He tried to swallow his tears but they were hard and lumpy.

'I can...' He said. 'I can go back to the stage.'

'And break down there?' Renu made an ugly grimace. 'What the fuck for?'

He looked down. And tried hard to swallow again.

The shack smelled of alcohol and stale sweat. It was an airless hole.

Renu drew him close. Her arms were around him, and the jungle of bangles. They jingled lightly. They could cut his skin, make it bleed.

'Tell me na,' she whispered. 'What are you hiding?'

'The prayer hall,' he whispered. 'I keep thinking of the prayer hall.'

'The prayer hall,' she repeated softly. 'And someone in there?'

Relief flooded him like a delirium. That he had told her. Of how he floated in the songs of prayer, huddled in thin cotton. How his eyes teared up in the smoke of incense. And other things.

How he came to love a pair of bony shoulders out there. How he came to play hide and seek with his love. How the shoulders shone heavenly light.

Renu milked stories out of him. Just the way she milked everything. When his eyes glistened she knew the tale that would go with it. When he stammered she knew what he did not want to say. When he looked away she knew exactly how he wanted her to prod him so that he would talk.

She was his nest. A bird with huge, soft wings.

'Someone in prayer?' She looked into his eyes. Did her eyes look wet?

Sharply, he looked away.

He nodded. Slowly, very slowly.

Swiftly, she pulled him around.

She cupped his face again.

'Go, Go, my son. Go back there,' she said. 'Let go,' she whispered. 'Go be happy.'

Her voice was hoarse. She kissed his forehead and drew away.

He stepped out of the shack. Behind him was the smell of booze and stale sweat.

Before him were Pir and Sana. Pir looked thunderstruck. Sana chewed on something, her eyes large and curious.

'Where are you going?' Pir asked him breathlessly.

'To...to the ashram,' He said as his voice faltered.

Pir spat on the ground. When he looked up, he was no longer a child. There was violence in his eyes.

Sana chewed on and stared at Yogi. Her eyes were those of a dead fish.

SrK packed Yogi's suitcase slowly and carefully. He placed the books at the bottom and then put the neatly folded clothes on top. Home clothes were rolled up in the corner. There was something womanlike about him.

'You will go, won't you?' He asked, his voice almost hard to hear.

Yogi nodded. SrK couldn't see him as his eyes were sunk in the suitcase. Yogi hoped he wouldn't see him. His heart was heavy, and warm with guilt. SrK had loved him, called out to him. He had said no.

SrK slid a jar of sweet aam pickle under Yogi's clothes.

'You are running away,' SrK said. 'You know that, don't you?'

Something steeled in Yogi, suddenly. Saffron is the colour of abandonment, isn't it?

'Boys go there and remain boys all their lives,' SrK said absently. 'They never leave. The brotherhood is overpowering.'

He wrapped Yogi's sports shoes in newspaper. Headlines stared at Yogi's face.

'My brothers got into the sports field,' he went on. 'The big grassy patch near the main gate. Running in circles. Playing football to get closer to God. Mobs of sweaty, muddy boys. Shepherding them to the haze of incense in the prayer hall.'

'The scent of sweaty, muddy boys,' his voice softened. 'They could never leave.'

Suddenly, SrK turned around.

'But what about Kajol?' He asked. 'He's such a smart student. Everybody's dream!'

'Kajol knows what he wants,' Yogi said calmly. But his heart beat wildly.

SrK squatted on the floor like an old woman. His eyes looked lost.

'You were special, Anirvan,' he said. 'I thought you were for the world.'

Yogi stared at him in silence.

The Colour of Desertion

He was the conscience and protector of the dynasty. Bhishma disentangled his colossal bow from his shoulder and reached for his quiver. He was a great silver man. Dressed in white and silver, his long white beard floating in the wind. His eyes looked like they belonged to a sad lion. They had a dull shine.

He was all-powerful. He had given up everything. No desire, no woman, no offspring, nothing of this world.

Bhishma reached for his quiver. The ancient patriarch of the Kaurava dynasty and the general of their army, who would die only when he wanted to die. No one could kill him against his wish.

They were in the battlefield and their flesh throbbed. They were not watching TV. They were not watching the long-running soap opera which brought to life their heroes from The Mahabharata exactly the way they imagined it. Silver Bhishma, a ferocious Karna and an agile Arjun.

The common room of Bliss Hall was a dark place. The TV was a small square of light that flickered in front. But they were all inside it, there on the battlefield.

Eighty boys from Class 9 sat huddled in the darkness, afraid to breathe. Kajol and Yogi sat at the back, next to the Lotus who sat on a chair behind them.

They held their breath. Bhishma was going to shoot missiles at Arjun. Grandsire Bhishma! Tremors shot through their flesh. The great ancient sage warrior was going to shoot the hell out of prettyboy Arjun dressed as a woman while the Pandavas served their hidden exile. Big sari-wrapped thighs and false long hair. Killer weapons tied to a tree like a corpse.

'Come,' Kamal Swami had said the moment they arrived. '*Mahabharat* is about to come on TV. Let's go watch.'

Kajol and Yogi followed him into the darkness of the common room. The boys were already there.

It was easy to forget everything there. There was darkness all around. There was only the shimmer of the television and the drama unfolding inside. They all knew the Pandavas were the good guys and they were exiled for no reason by the wicked Kaurava brothers, but who cared about all that when Grandsire Bhishma had pulled out a long deadly arrow and perched it on his bow.

That pansy prince who'd chickened out at the sign of the Kaurava army drove the chariot while Arjun, dressed as the eunuch who taught dance, twanged on his killer bow, the Gandiv.

They wanted the sad silver lion to win. To kill the long-haired eunuch. They longed for it because they knew it would not happen. That the long-haired eunuch was Arjun and all weapons in the universe were under his spell.

On his chariot, Bhishma frowned. The true man. The true king who never became king. The son of Holy Ganga.

He had renounced. He was a god.

Arjun! The pansy upstart eunuch!

Warmth crept on Yogi's skin. The warmth of flesh. Kajol's left hand was so close to his right hand that their hairs touched. Yogi could hear him breathe. His eyes were transfixed on Bhishma. Quickly, his chest rose and fell with his breath.

A mist grew inside Yogi's chest. It was no longer Bhishma on TV but Sachin Tendulkar. The prodigal child who hit every ball out of the stadium. He was absurd and they grew mad with excitement. Mad with excitement as Kajol's little-boy fingers curled inside Yogi's hand.

Time had stopped. For several years.

Today Yogi and Kajol's hands did not touch but breathed on one another. Their hair brushed against one another. Softly, they played, across Kamal Swami's taut saffron robe.

Their minds floated outside their bodies. Vanishing wisps of air. The last breath of a dead man.

SrK had nodded when Yogi said bye. But he wouldn't let Yogi see his eyes.

Yogi and Kajol sat in the sea of quietly breathing boys. There was no life in their bodies.

The man and the woman were vandalized statues. They looked lifeless. But their despair was muddy, dark and heavy, touched by life that had withered inside.

But the woman cried. The man was stone. His tears had stilled.

They were Kajol's parents.

Yogi's mother was there too. She looked at him. She fought blue shock to make sense of things. Her gaze floated all over him like a smooth reptile and tried to slip inside his clothes. She had cried too, but her tears had long dried.

His father wasn't there. He had a busy new life.

Twelve monks stood in a row. It had to be twelve whenever new initiates took the vows. Like the original twelve brothers who had set up the order. Right here in Uttarayan, north of Calcutta. They had lit the fire on these grounds and joined hands.

The fire was ready. It simmered slowly in the haze of the dusk.

'My boy!' Kajol's mother cried.

Kajol's father looked away. Vigorously, he shook his head. Something he couldn't bear to think about.

Kajol could have made the family proud. He would have made IIT proud with his brain. Famous American universities sat in wait for someone like him. His father, Kajol had told Yogi so many times, had the entire map in the palm of his hand. He was the man who always knew the whole story.

Kajol wanted to lose it all. Today he would.

Kajol didn't see them there.

The two of them sat beside the fire. They were shirtless and wore thin cotton dhotis. Prayer hall dhotis. They were so thin that mosquitoes bit them through the cloth. The Lotus sat across them.

Yogi held Kajol's hand and the whole world turned into liquid. He floated. How could a boy's hand be bony and soft at the same time? But Kajol was no longer a boy. He was almost eighteen.

For the next seven days, the ashram would give them no food. They had to go around the neighbourhood with a begging bowl. But in these lanes, all knew the new monks. For them it was a blessing to give alms to the monks.

At the end of seven days, they would return to their patron—Kamal Swami. He would give them the white robes. They would be brahmacharis. Men who walked the god-path.

The heat of the fire burned Yogi's eyes. He could not see his mother anymore. Across the fire, he saw his dead grandmother. She smiled.

'Seven generations before,' she cackled. 'And seven after.'

He tried to say something but could not.

'Nirvana for all,' she said and smiled. Her face was red in the light of the fire.

The Lotus started to hum the prayer. It was the song they sang every evening in the hostel. In the monk's lone voice, it sounded desolate.

Kajol and Yogi sat close to each other, their naked hands entwined. They had found peace.

Kamal Swami stopped. 'Twelve years,' he said. 'It will take you twelve years to earn saffron. The hue of Renunciation.'

'But I know you boys will earn it,' he smiled. 'I trust you.'

Yogi's fingers curled into Kajol's. The heat of their skin overpowered the heat of the smoldering fire. Their breath rose and fell together. Little lifeless toys simmering in the warm brine of sweat.

'One day everyone will learn to renounce,' the Lotus whispered. 'One day all will turn saffron.'

Kajol wrapped his arm around Yogi. A soft bony arm. He felt Kajol's nails scrape his flesh.

Yogi entered his hug and felt safe. His corpse melted into nirvana.

Thank You!

The Scent of God came to me like grace, a blessing unasked, whatever it is, a story, a sensation, a fragment of a memory, of things that never happened but did, a world real but invented. But if the raw stirrings were a personal epiphany, it arrived in the world through its own temples, through communities of the faithful, through love and support of many individuals, groups and institutions.

Wellesley College, for an idyllic Fellowship at the Suzy Newhouse Center for the Humanities, where much of the writing happened. The (then) director Anjali Prabhu for her enthusiasm about my work, and for being a consistent source of support and affection. The rich community of fellows there: Sandy Alexandre, Gurminder Bhogel, Hilary Chute, Tanalis Padilla, Jerry Pinto, Banu Subramanium. Mrinalini Chakravarty for making the trip from Virginia to Boston to lead the atelier discussion on the book-in-progress. Cory McMullen for administrative support. Eve Zimmerman and Sue Sours for hosting me.

Mike Rezendes for fabulous conversation in Colorado and Cambridge, for sharing unheard stories of *Betrayed* and *Spotlight*, for his support of this book.

More than anything else, Ashoka University, my intellectual and artistic home since 2016, my wonderful colleagues and students here. A very special debt to the Centre for Studies in Gender and Sexuality, directed by Madhavi Menon, for supporting me with a group of talented research and editorial assistants who were part of the making of this book, at different stages of the process. Ishan Chatterjee, Nandita Dutta, Samarth Menon, Govind Narayan, Prithvi Pudhiarkar, Suhasini Patni, Samvida Rungta, Pragnya Divakar, Karthik Shankar, and Manasa Veluveli—you've put much work in this book, and for that I'm deeply grateful. Shiv Dutt Sharma for facilitating it all.

At Ashoka, thanks also to Durba Chattaraj, Jonathan Gil Harris, and Mahesh Rangarajan for their support of my work, and their enthusiasm over it.

Friends on whom I can always count on to read my work and share responses both sharp and sympathetic:

Vivek Shanbhag, who heard my half-baked mutterings about this story long before a single sentence was written and shared excitement that happily, did not fade after he read an early draft that gained much from his feedback.

Amit Chaudhuri, for embodying the sixth sense of art. And all beyond that.

Saikat Chakraborty, reader, writer, scientist, friend, who reads everything I write and manages to infect an enthusiasm about it all that is hard to believe, every time.

Wendell Mayo, who sent me out in the world years ago from his Creative Writing Program in idyllic Ohio but who continues to be a support and a sounding board as if he's still in an office down the hall from me.

Old friends who took me back to the past to mine misty worlds: Somesh Bhattacharya, Kaushik Majumdar, Nilendu Misra. I owe you guys big time. In the same breath, Chandril Bhatacharya and Rajat Chaudhuri, denizens of the same past, nourishers of the future.

Sudip Ghosh, early reader, long-time patron, archive of everything that matters. Lopa Ghosh, friend, fellow writer, fellow parent, for reading all that I write. Warm, creative souls who have been friends to my books and its author: Jayita Sengupta, Maina Bhagat, Jhimli Mukherjee-Pandey, Keri Walsh, Ragini Tharoor-Srinivasan, Sohinee Roy, Suhrid Sankar Chattapadhyay, Kiranjeet Chaturvedi. Kindred souls in the book world who supported it in many way: Poulomi Chatterjee, Hansda Sowvendra Shekhar, Anurag Basnet, Arpita Das.

Mona Sengupta and Sushroota Sarkar, for faith and ever-contagious affection.

Pinaki De, for making so many of my books such things of beauty, and for the viscerally beautiful cover for this one.

Himanjali Sankar, for her heartfelt enthusiasm about my work, not only this one, which is her godchild, but also for work I've published before.

Sayantan Ghosh, for being that keen editor who straddles the sweet spot between the high and the deep, the light and the solemn—here's hoping the book has some of your wonderful spirit.

Rahul Srivastava for bringing this book to daylight. Abhay Singh and Bharti Taneja for spreading the word.

Three excerpts from the book saw daylight before

the rest. The first one appeared in *Caravan* Vantage. That excerpt came through a somewhat difficult history, during a time of many bitter incidents of violation of free speech and writing in the South Asian public sphere. I'm especially grateful to the people who stood by me at that time and supported the book's first utterance: Anjum Hasan, Dipanjan Sinha, Gita Hariharan, Nilanjana S. Roy, Hartosh Singh Bal, Jaya Bhattacharji-Rose, Sharon Marcus, PEN India and PEN Canada.

Arunava Sinha for conveying an early sample from a work-in-progress in *Scroll.in*. GJV Prasad for featuring another one in the final issue of *Muse India* edited by him.

This book owes is deepest debt to Subho. Without her biting discipline and bittersweet editorial love, it would have been a far lesser being.

Inaya, who is not allowed to read any of my books till she is ten, sixteen perhaps for this one; for helping me craft the blurb for this one, regardless. Neer, who is fast learning to read and write, for his endless curiosity and nonstop chatter about The Sent off God.

Thank you all.